by: Nolan "Dino" Hall

Transcribed & Edited by: Cheraee C.

Harm's Way:
Surviving The Wilderness

MOCY PUBLISHING
WWW.MOCYPUBLISHING.COM
Detroit, Michigan

Distributed by

4900 LaCross Road
North Charleston, SC 29406
USA

Harm's Way: Surviving The Wildness

ISBN 978-1-940831-08-4

Published by Mocy Publishing, LLC.
Website: www.mocypublishing.com
Email: info@mocypublishing.com
Phone: (313) 436-6944

HARM'S WAY
Surviving the Wilderness

Mud slide…

It looked like a blanket of mud about fifteen feet high violently pulling the trees from their roots moving along with timber, rocks, soil, and muck. This mixture of rubbish became part of this land monster. It moved fast down the mountain toward them. The night of it brought about gasps and screams.

The earth mixed with debris hit the side of the vehicle with head jerking force; practically covering the whole bus making the tires screech in protest to the sudden change in direction causing it to slowly teeter then tip tumbling down the mountain side over rocks and brush for what seemed to take forever. More screams with glass breaking accompanied with sounds of metal being crunched with each roll of the bus.

A group of twelfth graders and school staff members are traveling on their way to a long awaited trip to enjoy themselves at Yellowstone National Park, when a tragic accident leaves the survivors without transportation and shelter. Many miles are between them and civilization. The scenery of this vast country is beautiful, but it also proved to be equally as deadly. The elements and animals are not kind. What's left of the group make their way aimlessly about the great state of Wyoming's wilderness in search of being rescued. Hank and Michael do their best using their outdoor training and Boy Scout skills helping the group to get out of this in one piece. Trying to stay alive is a constant challenge as the group learns to live in a primitive state of existence. All of them come to realize if any of them are to survive this disastrous ordeal, they must learn to work together which makes them stronger than they would be apart.

Author's Note

This work of fiction was fueled with my thoughts of conflict, resolution, and the will to live because life isn't always easy. This story depicts helping others even when it brings us out of our comfort zone, even when we don't get a pat on the back for it because we help ourselves by helping others. Ralph Waldo Emerson said," success is knowing that someone else breathes easier because you have lived." Despite my hardship, it has served me well to think of more ways I can then I can't. There will always be someone who isn't happy unless you are sad. And there are those who will pray for you, and those who will prey on you. Remain positive and keep in mind that children invent excuses for failure and men/women produce strategies for success.

Best Regards

Nolan "Dino" Hall

Acknowledgments

Blessing, Honor, Glory, and Power onto an awesome

Creator, I give you praise.

Love and Embraces to my loved ones.

Barbara Bradley and Demetrius Favors, you both have my
love and appreciation for your unyielding friendship.

Crystal Thomas and my nieces' Aliviah and Ariana you all

are jewels.

Willie and Johnny Hawkins, I wish you well with brotherly

love.

My heartfelt love and blessings to the Traylor family.

Much love to Valerie and Nikeye' Embry.

Love and everlasting friendship to Veeda Randall.

Terri Fowles, wishing you well in Australia.

To: Our Boy/Girl Scouts of America

Never cease in your aspiration of excellence because your
labor of love helps to produce tomorrow's men and women
of integrity.

To: Our American Military

You've given so much; your worth could never be measured. I salute you with heartfelt honor and much respect.

To: Our Law Enforcement, First Responders, and all

who are in Authority:

Thank you for your sacrifices, selfless endeavors, and willingness to help others. I've learned much from you.

Chapter 1:

Michael sat there at his desk with pencil in hand, hovering above the test that he wasn't prepared for. He was just a half inch over six feet with medium length blond hair on a medium frame. He took a quick look around the classroom as the other students were deeply engrossed finishing work on their test, racing to beat the clock as time was running out. The teacher Mr. Wilson sat behind his desk ruffling through some papers, checking the time on his watch and looking at the students in his class from time to time. Michael's mind seemed to wonder as he gazed out the window.

It was early spring with the sun shining and the weather was perfect for being outside. Yet here he sat in this classroom, the last place on earth he wanted to be. His thoughts went to the girl who sat at the desk in front of his. Amanda was her name; a pretty name for a pretty girl. She had long brown hair, and today she wore it in two brads.

Michael couldn't help, but to close his eyes and breathe in the sweet smell of the bubble gum Amanda was chewing. The two went on their first date last week, and the furthest he had gotten was a kiss. The relationship was just beginning as girlfriend and boyfriend. There was still a lot to learn about each other he couldn't put his finger on it. She made him feel crazy inside and he embraced it wanting more. But the excitement of that kiss had a lot of hang time because it felt as if it just happened today. He noticed she was moving right along through the test without hesitation. Then he was brought back to reality by someone tapping on his back with a pencil. It was his best friend Hank who was sitting right behind him. Hank was just as tall as Michael with just a bit more mass on his frame, an African American who wore his hair short with brush waves. They had pretty much grown up together all of their lives and now here they were in the 12th grade together.

"Stop doing nothing, and start doing something. Don't just sit there Michael," whispered Hank.

Michael turns to his seat to face Hank, "I'm trying, but my thoughts seem to be divided right now."

"Michael you know how important this test is to our grade man you got to pull it together. Someone else heard their conversation and decided to butt in.

"You lame, I'll bet you didn't even study for the test. Your too much like your old man. What is he anyway a scout master? Into that outdoor boy scout crap," said a voice in the seat behind Hank. It was Keith, the school's bully, who was bigger than most teenagers his age. Keith was six feet two inches, had curly brown eyes, with a barrel chest. He looked boarder line fat with muscles and he always wore clothes one size too small to accent his size.

"Keep my father out of your mouth fluffy!" Michael snarled louder then he realized causing some of the students to laugh. Keith looked at those who were laughing with threatening eyes which caused them to stop and lower their eyes.

"Shut up before I come up there and beat your…" Michael noticed the surprised look on Hank and Keith's face and how quick they both on cue suddenly ignored Michael and acted as if they were doing the test they had already finished. Michael knew what that meant so he turned back around to face the front of the class only to find Mr. Wilson coming his way fast.

"Mr. Winchester, I couldn't help, but notice you were turned around in your seat talking or copying the answers from Mr. Miles. You know the rules; zero tolerance while testing. Now remove yourself and report to the office," said the teacher.

"Mr. Wilson, look at my test you can see I haven't even wrote anything down yet!"

"It's non-negotiable; go to the office and you, the principal, and I are going to have a little talk." Michael grabbed his backpack and headed for the door. When he

opened the door he looked back at Hank who noticed the

word with his mouth silently "sorry." Amanda was looking

at Michael with folded arms and a disappointed look on her

face still chewing her gum. Michael closes the door and

heads to the principal's office. He could hear Mr. Wilson's

voice saying, "pencils down, time is up,"

*

The school board had agreed months ago to start the

annual trip early morning to Yellowstone National Park

since it was a good ways away. All was accounted for when

the bus took off some hours ago from Boulder, Colorado.

They took Interstate 25 crossing the Wyoming state line

many miles back. Once they got off 1-25 the bus took some

back roads through the valleys traveling through the great

state of Wyoming. Lightning splits the pre-dawn sky

briefly illuminating mountains from miles around bringing

with it a mild rain descending across the land. Some of the

students shielded their eyes while others averted their attention from the blinding brightness of the powerful force of nature that webs its way across the sky. The sound that follows is a roaring thunder. Weeks of melting snow and the precipitation on the mountain causes some streams to swell. The overflow causes water to mix with dirt, rocks, and timber that gives way to gravity creating a mudslide now tumbling down the mountainside.

*

The two teachers were Mr. Wilson and Mrs. Artis. They were drinking coffee and talking with the school's bus driver Mrs. Mayers. They didn't think it necessary to turn the bus around traveling through this peaceful valley since this storm appeared non-threatening with the mild rain so they decided to proceed with the trip as planned. The sixteen students were very excited about traveling through the beautiful country. The awesome sights of the big trees, lakes, valleys, and rock formations were breath-taking. Michael sat there looking out the window as the school bus made its way through the valley. He couldn't help, but to think how he almost didn't make this trip. The principal wasn't happy about seeing Michael in his office, but the punishment came down to either being suspended from school and not graduate or stay after school, do the test, and some additional homework that his teacher Mr. Wilson deemed appropriate. The choice was simple, he definitely wanted to graduate and being able to go on this long, awaited trip, and to spend time with Amanda was at the top of his list along with graduating. There she sat on the right, fourth seat from the front with her friend Mae and her other female friends sitting across opposite isles from where she sat.

When he got on the bus, his friend Hank was already sitting there. Keith, the bully sat directly behind Amanda and every time Michael tried to look to the front of the bus at Amanda, Keith's big head and thick neck blocked the view.

"Stop rubber necking; you can't see her from here with Shamu the whale in the way," said Hank.

"Nothing beats a failure, but a try. You know how we eagle scouts do it." Saying that made Hank think how far Michael and him had went back growing up in the middle class as next door neighbors. Their fathers worked together at a factory which had brought their families closer. Michael's dad had been a scout leader for years teaching children the American Boy Scout way so it wasn't by chance that they both had joined the boy scouts together and came up through the ranks reaching the highest honor; eagle scout. The American Boy Scouts was known for their courage, honor, and willingness to help others. Hank had hopes of someday becoming a scout leader like Michael's dad. Hank's thoughts were interrupted by Michael.

"Hank what's up with you and Mae? I saw her sitting up front with Amanda when I came on the bus. I haven't heard you speak about her since we've been on this trip. I can tell you love her as much if not more than I do Amanda so what's up with the two of you?" Hank and Mae had been a couple for some time now. Mae had confessed her love to him weeks ago. He loved her, but he had never told her. Hearing Michael saying he loved her made Hank a little uneasy; he said something in a low voice, too low for Michael to hear, "I can't hear you Hank, let me guess Mae not only has your heart she got your tongue too?" Michael asked loudly getting some laughs from people who were within ear shot. Michael smiled having fun with his friend. Hank was embarrassed, but knew he had it coming with all the cheap shots he constantly took at Michael. Michael saw that Hank was pointing his finger at the seat in front of him, but before Michael could catch on a female's head appeared over top of the seat that was in front of theirs. It was Mae!

"Hi, Michael," said Mae. She was a beautiful, young woman with coal black dread locks that looked nice hanging past her shoulders.

"Hello Mae, Hank and I were just talking about you," said Michael trying to play it off and not act surprised.

"Mae you never heard me mention the word love," said Hank trying hard to conceal his true feelings that confused him. He had a problem processing the feelings he had when Mae looked at him. He couldn't say it was love because he had never experienced love other then love of family, but with her it was as if being around her made him short of breath and his heart raced faster. He was experiencing these things right now as she looked into his eyes. She was more of the aggressor in their relationship.

She was raised around six brothers so she liked being a tomboy.

"Baby, that's okay you didn't have to say it you were thinking it. Not to worry, I'll find some way to bring you out of your shyness. I asked you at that rest stop to come up here and sit with me, but no you wanted to sit back there with your friend, no offense Michael."

"None taken Mae, Hank you knew he was sitting in front of us this whole time?"

"Yeah, we've been reaching around the seat doing the touchy feel with our hands from time to time," Hank said with a dreamy look in his eyes.

"I just find it hard to believe Mae has been sitting there the whole time and I didn't know it. Wait a minute, what rest stop?" Michael asked still trying to train his eyes on Amanda, but still no luck. All he could see was the back of other students' heads that were doing their thing viewing the sights, texting, or talking on their phones, but still no Amanda.

"We stopped and stretched our legs miles back when you were sleep. I didn't wake you because I knew you were tired behind doing those battery of tests you stayed late at school doing last night. Anyway that's when they traded seats with the people who were sitting in front of me," said Hank. Michael was thinking to himself as he wished
Hank had awakened him so he could use the rest room.

"Michael, you should know that I was trying to surprise you with…" Before he could finish his sentence a female voice said, "me!" Amanda's head appeared next to Mae's in the seat in front of him.

"I was trying to tell you Amanda was sitting there with Mae," Michael was surprised and awe struck.

"Michael, I heard what you said. I love you too and its okay we can talk later in private if that's okay with you."

"Yeah, I would feel more comfortable with that Amanda. How about that, I was just looking for you up there, and here you are." Michael didn't say it, but was thankful she gave him a way out in front of Mae and Hank.

The bus driver noticed small forest debris started to fall to the road from the upper part of the mountain.

"I'm gonna have to ask you children to sit down in your seats back there," yelled Mrs. Mayers from the front of the bus seeing the girls from the rear view mirror. Amanda and Mae rolled their eyes at the bus driver for calling them children, but did as they were told. The two couples talked for a while when Mae suggested that Michael switch seats with her so she could be with Hank and he could be with Amanda. They did the switch and the moment they sat down beside her was a strange eerie noise.

It was a rumbling sound accompanied by cracking with the snapping of wood and boulders moving against another. Some female screamed and then everyone saw it. It looked like a blanket of mud about fifteen feet high. It was violently pulling the trees from their roots moving along with timber, rocks, and various things that were picked up from the land moving fast down the mountain the bus was traveling up. Gasps and screams filled the bus. Mrs. Mayers knew she must do something, but accidently slammed on the brakes making the bus fish tail, crashing against the guard rail. She attempted to put the bus in reverse to avoid this moving land monster, but to no avail gears were grinding with many of the students starting to freak out panicking by standing up trying to run off the bus wanting to be anywhere, but here. Others were putting on seat belts that should have already been on. The bus driver frantically got the bus in gear and stomps down on the accelerator. Tires spun, but the bus doesn't move. Hank yelled, "keep your feet planted on the floor and make yourselves into a ball. Brace for impact!" Those that heard made themselves into a ball, which unknowingly saved some lives. The earth mixed with debris hit the side of the bus with head jerking force, partially engulfing the bus making the tires on the bus screech in protest to the sudden change in direction. This caused the bus to slowly tip then tumble down the mountain side over rocks and brush for what seemed to take forever. There was more screams and glass was breaking, and the sounds of metal being crunched with each roll of the bus. The massive amount of mud that followed them down this mountain cushioned most of the impact, and those who weren't wearing their seatbelts were thrown around like rag dolls. The bus came to its final resting place on its wheels slightly tipped against a large oak tree at the base of the mountain, partially submerged in the mud that followed it down. What was left of the mudslide slowly slid

from the mountain and disbursed in the forest and valley
below.

Chapter 2

Mr. Wilson awoke to the loud sound of the engine revving; the tires on the bus were still spinning. People were crying and moaning from the pain, and some were still unconscious. Wilson's head was aching from being banged around. He was a short man in his late fifties, had overweight fat around the mid-section which earned him the name among the students of being shaped like a pear. He was bald on top with little hair on the sides; this accounted for comb over hair style he always wore to hide some of his baldness. At the present his hair was disheveled giving him the appearance of a crazy man. Once he gathered his senses he looked around for others he could help. Some were thrown about the bus; some were conscious and others were still unconscious, but most are still being held in their seats by the seatbelt. Wilson unbuckled his seatbelt to go check on the others. Upon closer inspection of Mrs. Artis, she didn't make it. Her skinny frame was twisted in an unnatural position for the human body. Mrs. Mayers the bus driver wasn't in her seat; evidence supported she was thrown out the window. The windshield was broken out, but the jagged parts of glass had blood around the opening. He banged his head and took a moment to reflect on the loss of life then he reached for the ignition and shut the engine off. Looking around the bus, he saw the backdoor opened with students helping students out of the damaged bus. The rain had finally stopped, but he could feel the cold. Wilson stumbled his way down the aisle to help who he could; some he awakened and directed to exit out the back. Some he saw he knew would never wake up again; he checked for their pulse anyway. Then he went back to the front to radio for help, but the radio was dead. As he neared the back Michael and Hank extended their hands to help him off. Wilson thanked those who wore instrumental in helping others. Wilson asked them all to gather in a circle right there at the rear of the bus to listen to him. First, he told them to remain calm while he did a head count. They started out on their trip with sixteen students, two teachers, and one bus driver making it nineteen that got on the bus. Now among the living was seven students and himself; a total of eight who got off the bus. Looking at the wreckage; Wilson considered himself lucky; some would even say blessed. How anyone could survive what they just went through was beyond him. He took a look up to see just how far they had fallen and couldn't see the road up on the mountain; vegetation was thriving as far as it limited his eyes to see. The sun was starting to rise; maybe he could see better in a few minutes he thought to himself. Some were crying and others were moaning from pain. He took his phone out and pushed the numbers 911; the phone display showed NO SERVICE!

"Okay, now listen up; I need you all to be calm so we can get through this. Whoever has their cell phones I want to call for help."

"Mine is somewhere on that bus with my purse," said Amanda.

"Mine too," answered Mae. They didn't want to go back on that bus to do so would mean revisiting that horrid scene. Michael and Hank left theirs at home; they were use to camping with the scouts without phones.

"I have one!" Said a girl named Beth.

"I…. have one too, but you must get it from…my pocket; I believe my fingers on my right…. hand is broke," said a skinny young man named Van. He held his hand close to his chest due to the pain he was in. None of the phones was of any use; one the battery was drained and the other one showed no service.

"We're probably in a dead zone," said Hank.

"Dead zone, you got that right my dark-skinned bro. Look around you; pretty much everything around you is dead or dying. We all are going to die; this whole trip sucks!" Yelled Keith with his hands cupped to his mouth as he shouted it to the morning sky. Beth started to cry; Amanda and Mae looked at Keith with disgust and went to comfort her. Van was still moaning from the injured hand.

Keith walked up to Van. "Damn man your whimpering like a girl; I banged my head and lost my phone in that damn bus somewhere you don't see me being a girl about it."

"Keith leave him alone!" Michael said.

"Or what? You ain't going to do nothing about it," Keith said with squinting his eyes.

"Stop it! The both of you; Keith I'm in charge here stop creating problems and watch your language. Am I clear?" Wilson warned.

29

Keith said nothing and Wilson knew Keith would act out again it was just a matter of time. Keith walked a little ways off complaining out loud how the adults got them all into this mess and about them being here in this ankle deep mud and how their situation sucked. Mr. Wilson leaned against a tree for support; he was starting to feel light-headed and didn't have the energy to deal with Keith at the moment. Michael noticed Hank was cradling his left arm and went to his friend's side.

"How bad is it Hank?"

"I'm not a doctor, but if I had to guess it feels like it might be dislocated." A howl is heard off in a distance that gets everyone's attention.

"What the hell was that?"

"Watch your mouth young man. Whatever it is its way out there; we're here safe, cold, but safe," said Wilson trying to be a strong leader and keep the students reassured and under his authority.

"With all due respect Mr. Wilson, we should be looking for some type of shelter and then build a fire. Everyone is cold and some wet; we run the risk of hypothermia if we don't get to some heat soon," explained Michael.

"We must stay here; they will come looking for us. How can they find us if we don't stay put?" Wilson said. Hank chimed in," Mr. Wilson that could be days; they have no way of knowing that we were in an accident or where we are and people are hurt and dead; we should be moving on."

"Listen, I know you all are wet, cold, and scared, but I believe we should build the fire around here somewhere so why the big rush to move on from where?" Wilson said. They heard the howl again only this time closer with another howl from the opposite direction. The whole group began looking around in all directions, but couldn't see anything in this thick forest.

"Because what we're hearing is a wolf or wolves they often travel in packs to wear their prey down even after chasing them for miles. They may be trying to, out flank us right now had just because we can't see them don't mean that they can't see us," explained Michael. Saying that made everyone even more paranoid especially Keith; he started to back away from their small group.

"I think I'll just wing it on my own and get away from you losers."

"Keith, whatever you do don't run; we should all stick together; there is strength in numbers," stated Hank. Keith stopped and looked hard at Hank.

"Your advice is noted and ignored my dark-skinned home boy." Hank couldn't take any more of his verbal assaults.

"Your hopeless man; I'll bet you act like an idiot because you come from a broken home. Your parents were broke, the T.V. was broke, refrigerator was broke, and your father broke his foot off in your ass." For the first time since the accident a few in the group let out a little laugh even Wilson thought Keith needed a bit of his own verbal abuse. Then he butted in, "Hank watch your language."

"Before this is over I'll be the one to break my foot off in your ass," replied Keith walking towards Hank. Hank gets in a stance to fight even with his dislocated arm still hanging limp at his side. Michael steps in between them, "now ain't the time for this; we're being hunted."

"So what if we are being hunted; I can handle myself and I know how to fight. You better get out of my face before you find out," warned Keith.

"SHUT UP!" Wilson yelled.

"Stop all of this bickering; something is out there and you guys want to fight. All of you are young adults please start acting like it."

"So what am I suppose to do hang around here with these lames? You guys suck!" Keith said pointing to Michael.

"No, by all means don't hang around us so go on out there tough guy or shut up and stop complaining. I know your scared like the rest of us, but your way of hiding it, and dealing with it is to act tough; no one cares if your tough out here," Michael retorted. This really had Keith mad so he charged Michael as soon as the two locked arms they all heard and saw someone or something stumble through the brush right into their view. Michael and Keith separated and looked at what everyone else was looking at. It was the bus driver Mrs. Mayers; she was bloody from being thrown through the windshield. She could see the group and started towards them dragging what seemed to be a broken leg.

She had small cuts on her face and neck. Her clothing was torn; the cut over her eyebrow was leaking blood in her eyes that she continued to wipe. The group went to meet her with hopes of helping her along. Keith stood there watching not sure what to do. She was about fifty yards out when they heard the barking that sounded like several of them. The realization that these canines were hunting Mrs. Mayers was evident when the group saw the wolves on her heels. The female bus driver knew they were after and she tried to run, but the smell of blood peaked their prey drive. The lead wolf took her down and the rest joined in on her. She screamed; growls could be heard and Mrs. Mayers screamed no more. The group stopped and couldn't believe what they were seeing; Beth, Amanda, and Mae screamed.

Wilson yelled, "no!" Hank and Michael was shouting at the wolves trying to get them to stop attacking Mrs. Mayers. Van joined in with Michael and Hank shouting at the wolves from a distance hoping they would stop, but their screams meant nothing to the beast when hunger had been with them for days. Keith knew she was dead or dying; no one could survive such an attack. The realization that those wolves and who knows what else out there may kill them all gave Keith a whole new prospective. They all were glued to the sight and frozen there with fear until one of the wolves looked up from their eating frenzy and saw the group some yards away. This wolf gave the group a hard look; its back went rigid. The hackles went up and it showed menacing sharp teeth growling; saliva mixed with blood dripped from the mouth. Michael holds out his arms so that no one goes beyond him and says, "everyone slowly back away," They did so not taking their eyes off the wolves; after getting some distance away they could still see the wolves. Beth broke the group's formation and ran.

"Beth no!" Michael shouted.

Predatory animals' natural instinct is to chase their prey; Beth's running kicked in the wolf's prey drive that was looking at them so he gave way to the chase.

"You guys stay together and RUN!" Michael said as he picked up a fallen branch. Wilson said, "I'll stay with you."

"No, you won't you can barely stand now GO!" Wilson left with the group; Hank looked back at his friend that he wished he could help. He knew Michael wouldn't allow him to stay to help and it would only waste time arguing with him trying to help in his condition would probably give them both killed. Michael would try to hold off the wolf to buy them some time; it's what he would have done if it wasn't for his arm. The group had gone through the brush; good now all he had to do was to survive this. Michael considered it a blessing that only this one wolf was in pursuit; the odds are better with this one than the whole pack. Michael didn't believe himself to be brave.

What gave him the strength right now was this scripture he remembered reading something about God giving man authority over animals or something like that. The wolf was charging in like he suspected and from what he knew about canines they would either go for a man's arms or the throat. His bet was the wolf would go for the kill which means it would leap for his throat. Michael stood like he was going to bat a ball at a baseball game; then he remembered that he had always struck out at bat.

Chapter 3

The group was running frantically through the brush; thorns pricked at them. Their breathing became labored; Amanda stopped abruptly when she reached a clearing, feeling bad for leaving Michael behind. Mae stayed alongside Amanda and knew without being told what was on her friend's mind. "Amanda no! You will get yourself killed!"

"I can't just leave him like that."

"I know, but what can we do?" Mae asked.

Wilson came running up behind them.

"Where is everyone?" Wilson asked.

"Beth and Van were together running that way," Mae said pointing in a westerly direction. And then Mae asked, "where is Hank? I thought you all were together." Wilson was bent over with his hands on his knees trying to catch his breath.

"Hank, I don't know, but we must keep moving before those wolves come after us," Wilson said in between breaths.

"You guys go on, I'm going back to help Michael," said Amanda giving them her back as she began to go the way she came. Wilson straightened himself up to stop her. Mae tapped his shoulder to get his attention. He stopped in his tracks and turned to face her.

"Where my b.f.f. goes, I go." Then she ran past him and caught up to Amanda. Wilson then ran to the front of them sweating profusely. "You two are coming with me and we are leaving now!" Wilson said loudly as he grabbed both girls arms and heads in the opposite direction they were headed. He slows; his grip on their arms weakens and he crumbles to the ground unconscious. They look down at him with concern and then at each other, flabbergasted.

*

Michael stood ready feet planted; the wolf was coming in hard and fast. He swings with all of his might barely missing the animal's head and by doing so he overextended himself. The wolf hits him high on his right shoulder and bites at his neck. The Eagle Scout goes down; force of the blow saves him by propelling him out the way of the canine's bite. He hits the ground and rolls over quickly on his back raising the branch with two hands to block the bite. The wolf locks on to the branch only inches from his face, shaking its head from side to side trying to rip the branch from the struggling man's hand, growling, and pushing itself closer to his face. Its front paws were on his chest; claws ripping his coat. The Eagle Scout was assaulted by the creature's foul, putrid breath, but didn't dare to turn his head away from the smell, must keep his eyes on this beast, and get up off this ground somehow. Michael yells in the canine's face with hopes of scaring this beast off of him; this only enrages the wolf to thrash about, and bite even harder on the branch that separated its teeth from his face. To the young man's surprise the branch breaks in two; the wolf rears up, and comes back down for its intended prey's throat. Being in survival mode, Michael instinctually pushes up with the two jagged pieces of wood to hold the beast off of him. The sharp wood pierces the wolf's hide; it continues to go for the kill even with the two pieces of wood in its hide. The claws make it through the Eagle Scout's coat and draws blood; he wenches from the pain just when he begins to tire with his strength about spent. Out of nowhere he sees a blur of wood that hits the wolf in its face; it yelps and rolls off the young man. Particles of bark from the limb got into Michael's eyes; it stings so he closes them and attempts to rub the debris out. Not being able to see he hears growling and sudden movement; now a thud hitting flesh that's accompanied by a yelp from the wolf. Michael finally clears his eyes and sees Hank standing toe to paw with the wolf swinging a limb with the one good hand connecting from time to time. The two jagged pieces of wood were no longer in the wolf; blood stains showed its skin was punctured, but not enough to slow it down. Michael gets up and grabs a long stick, and joins Hank in putting the canine down. The wolf gave it his all, but could not withstand the blows it received. The young men kept hitting the wolf until it moved no more. Sweat covered them and they were breathing hard. They stopped taking in big gulps of breath and give each other smiles of triumph and hugged with their sticks still in hand.

*

Van and Beth ran for their lives; both were very scared. Beth continues looking back from time to time not aware she's running under a low branch of a tree. One of its leaves slapped the young woman in the face causing her to stumble into Van bumping him so he extended his injured hand to help Beth up. As she grabbed his hand, Van yelled from the pain and pulled his hand back causing her to fall back to the ground. He cradled his hand regretting he offered that hand for help. She gets to her feet on her own, brushing the pine needles and leaves from her clothes. Then they realized that all could be heard was their heavy breathing. Something else occurred to them; they were no longer being chased.

*

Hank and Michael made their way to the clearing and seen Amanda and Mae on their knees over Mr. Wilson. He was out cold with the girls trying to revive him. Both girls jumped when they heard the boys approach them from the rear, "it's only us, what happened to him?" Michael asked pointing to Wilson. Both girls ran to their arms and gave them tight hugs.

"He just fell out, we don't know why. He hasn't responded to any of our attempts to revive him," answered Mae.

"I'm glad you two are safe," said Amanda.

"We were worried about the both of you also," Michael replied.

"Hey Wilson doesn't look so good," observed Hank. The boys let go of the girls and bent down to have a look at Wilson. They to be checked his pulse and breathing just then they heard a twig snap to their right. Both men stood immediately in defense positions with Wilson, Amanda, and Mae at their backs. They couldn't make the figure out for the thick vegetation until he stumbled into the clearing; it was Keith. He was a bit confused and seemed to be wondering about aimlessly. He had a small gash on his head that was slightly bleeding. His brown hair was disheveled going in all directions. His appearance was that of a crazed man as he stumbled into the clearing paranoid looking behind him from time to time and just fell down completely out of breath. He lay there on his back looking up at the others.

"Boy… am I…glad to see…you guys!" Keith managed to say in between breaths his body so desperately needed.

"Keith have you seen the others?" Hank asked.

"Hell no, I've been running for my life from those hungry wolf dogs."

Michael tore a piece from the lower part of his shirt; Hank knew what his friend was doing and did the same. Michael bent down and started to wipe the blood from Keith's head; Keith swatted Michael's hand away. The girls didn't understand why these two was tearing their shirts to help Keith when Mr. Wilson was clearly in worse shape and Keith showed he didn't want to help.

"Michael, why help someone who doesn't want help?" Amanda asked.

"Besides, Mr. Wilson needs you guys help more than his," Mae chimed in.

Before Michael could answer Hank jumped in, "because the smell of that blood will bring those wolves and who knows what other predators down on us. If we don't get rid of that scent of blood somehow Wilson and the rest of us won't make it through the night." The harsh reality washed over them like a wave.

"What are you waiting on? Get this stuff off of me!" Keith exclaimed. Michael removed what he could quickly and then Hank wrapped Keith's head covering the wound with what he had torn from his shirt.

"We don't have the time to build a fire and burn it or bury it. You guys stay here and I'll take this bloody cloth far away from us; animals have a keen sense of smell. You guys keep your eyes and ears open," Michael said as he took off through the woods.

"Be careful!" Amanda shouted. Hank looked around at their position and what was available to help them.

"What we could be doing is getting ready to move when Michael gets back," said Hank.

Keith stood to his feet and said," I'm a bit light-headed from tripping and cutting my head on a rock, but I can move. What about that poor lame there?" He indicated Wilson who was still unconscious on the ground.

"We can make what's called a travois; it's something the plains Indians used. It's a primitive vehicle used to transport someone who's hurt or can't walk," Hank explained.

"A what?" Both of the girls said at once.

"How do we make this vehicle? The only thing out here is woods and plants, Keith explained.

"Exactly, we make a platform made by two poles and netting. Keith I need you and the girls to break off two branches from that tree that's long enough to support Wilson's body and I will do what I can with my one good arm to find us some vines. We should be okay as long as we stay in sight of each other.

"Hold it, who made you boss to delegate who does what? And why can't you go break a branch?" Keith asked. The girls looked at Keith in disbelief.

"My arm is still dislocated, Keith if you have a better idea then let's hear it. Time is not on our side." Hank knew they didn't have the time for arguing and Wilson was in need of medical help. He remembered his Boy Scout oath: to help people at all times. He must find a way to get Keith on board with that, besides they could use his strength.

"Okay, I guess we'll do it your way this time, but I must say it again this sucks!" Keith complained. Amanda whispered something in Mae's ear and they both went over to Keith and each grabbed one of his hands.

"Okay, big boy we can all agree that this sucks so all we have to do is survive the suck," said Mae as they led him towards the tree to break his and their branches.

Chapter 4

The girls had sweet talked Keith into breaking their branch along with his. Hank had found and brought back a vine long enough to suit their purpose to move Wilson. Michael returned in time to help make the travois; it looked crude being made from wood and vine, but it would have to make do. Only a few hours of daylight remained as the sun descended giving way to the evening. The wind brought lower temperatures to the great state of Wyoming as six figures were outlined by the beautiful sun setting sky. The plan was to get to the mountain they seen a good ways off and this would give them a better vantage point to view miles around them. They traveled rugged terrain with no signs of civilization. Finally, coming upon grassland with plenty of high grass and other kinds of vegetation, but mostly trees, they moved in search for shelter keeping an eye out for danger. The eagle scouts made a mental note of the area they had been traveling, remembering the way they had come; keeping in mind that the wolves could still be on their trail. The constant threat plagued them that some wolf or any wild animal could jump out of concealment and try to make a meal of them at any time. The mosquito's were relentless, no matter how they swatted and killed them more would take their place. Wilson was still unconscious and tied to the roughly made transportation he was now being carried on. They stopped to rest from time to time traveling for close to two hours. Michael and Hank stressed the importance of them finding shelter and building a fire, because everyone was wet and cold. To get hypothermia out here would be a death sentence; no one would make it too long to these conditions being exposed to the elements. Keith and Michael were carrying the unconscious man and then Keith seen it.

"What's that up there?"

"Where?" Everyone said together hoping it wasn't anything life threatening. Keith set the end of the travois down he was carrying and pointed. Everyone seen it about two stories up from the foot of the mountain was a hole in one of the giant rock formations that seemed assessable to the sure footed. There were places where small rocks protruded out of the soil which could allow foot holds, but you still had to be careful of your footing. The land mass elevated up to what appeared to be a cave. Michael went up alone to check things out and make sure it was safe for the others. The angle of the climb was a bit steep; his foot slipped on the loose pebbles causing him to lose his balance and go rolling down the foot of the mountain landing at the feet of the others. Keith started to laugh when the pebbles followed Michael down peppering Keith and the others. They all ducked for cover shielding themselves with their arms over their heads until the pebble shower stopped. In all the confusion no one gave thought to shield Mr. Wilson. When they looked at him he was okay with only some small pebbles on him. Hank extended his good hand helping his friend up.

"You okay?" Amanda asked.

"Yeah it's a piece of cake," said Michael a bit shaken from the fall as he dusted himself off and headed back up giving it a second try. The others stood farther back at what they guessed to be a safe distance from anything falling on them. Michael learned quickly the key was not to walk directly in a straight line, but to walk in a zigzag pattern. Once there, he noticed it was a cave with a small entrance, but wide enough to go in two at a time. Part of the land was kind of flat at the mouth of this cave; it extended out to about a five foot lip that seemed to go around the mountain. Although, the mountain went much farther up it didn't seem accessible from where he stood. The cave was facing west; evidence of this was proven as the light from the setting sun flooded the cave. Michael could gage the distance inside to be roughly forty feet to the back, about thirty from side to side, and about twenty feet high with some animal bones and feces that had been here for a while. Some small bush plants had started to grow in the cracks of the cave's floor. The whole inside was oval-shaped as if when this giant rock was lava, a big air bubble was trapped inside and when the lava cooled it made this cavity inside the rock thousands of years ago making this what we know as a cave. No animal was present; Michael's face lit up with a smile knowing they could mend and rest up here. Michael went to the mouth of the cave and gave them the thumbs up and went down and told them it was safe for now. They all were careful of their footing; Michael and Keith brought Wilson up from behind with Hank in front of them the girls went in the cave first and both started backing up suddenly, but frantically rubbing their hands over their faces with eyes closed. The girls came close to running into those behind them. No one wanted to tumble down the mountain side.

"Girls stop!" Hank yelled. The girls stopped, but were still swatting at their faces loudly making high-pitched squealing noises. Hank got within reach of them telling them to stay still. Everyone wondered what was going on. After closer inspection, Hank noticed it was a big spider web on both of their faces along with dead bugs that couldn't escape the powerful contact of the web. Hank removed what he could with his one good arm. The girls finally opened their eyes," its okay, just a spider web," said Hank with a comforting voice.

"What the hell man! Can we go inside now? Wilson is getting very heavy," Keith complained. They made it inside the cave the girls apologized for the scare and Michael reassured them no one got hurt and more important things needed attention, pointing to the unconscious man. The girls went to do what they could by keeping Wilson warm on the floor of the cave by rubbing

Wilson's arms trying to warm him up. Everyone was cold, hungry, and tired. Their clothes being damp didn't help.

"We must build a fire," suggested Michael.

"To build a fire we need some things to make a fire. Look I'll begin to clean and clear this stuff out of the cave. I'm beat and need to get warm and rest up a bit which means you two go for the wood, "said Keith while pointing at Hank and Michael.

"We can't get warm without a fire Keith. Michael, I can't go another minute with this arm the way it is. Can you help me to put it back in place where I can be of more help," Hank asked.

"Are you sure? You know it's gonna hurt something awful," replied Michael.

"Yes I'm sure, let's get it over with."

"Okay, lay on your side." Hank did so and mentally prepared for the pain. Michael gently raised Hank's dislocated arm and put his foot under Hank's armpit for leverage.

"On the count of four brace yourself. One…" Suddenly Michael pushed down with his feet while at the same time quickly pulling upwards with the arm. There was a subtle pop. The pain was intense followed with a yell that was so loud it hurt all of their ears in the small cave going out through the valley causing some birds to fly from some trees. Hank remained on the floor of the cave squirming a bit, moaning loudly. Mae let go of Wilson's arm and attempted to go to Hank. Michael extended his arm blocking her and said, "let him ride it out Mae he'll be okay." After the pain subsided Hank managed to sat up and look around at the others. Michael then helped Hank to his feet then Mae rushed Hank throwing her arms around him.

"You gonna be okay baby?" Mae asked.

"Yes, I'll be fine," says Hank as he's swinging his arm in a circular motion rejoicing for the use of the arm again. He gave Mae a big hug and a kiss on her forehead and turned to his lifelong friend.

"I thought you said on the count of four!"

"No one ever goes on four," Michael replied.

"Thank you Michael, that hurt something bad, but it was well worth it. Thanks again man."

"Before you break your arm patting me on the back let's go find some wood to make a fire. It was Amanda's turn to go to Michael's arms and they hugged."

"You guys go; we'll do what we can to keep Wilson warm."

"Keith, can you keep watch over things," Keith gave a grunt.

"Oh and save the feces!" Hank said giving his dimpled smile as him and Michael neared the cave's exit.

"Man, why the hell should I save some damn animal dung?"

"Because it has a longer burn than wood and it'll aide in keeping us warm when we build the fire," answered Hank. Keith looked at him and Michael and walked to the back of the cave throwing his hands up and shaking his head. The scouts made their way down the mountain bringing the travois with them to carry wood back to camp. Their knives would have come in handy now, but like everything else the trusty knives were back on the bus. After some time the boys were headed back up the mountain to camp with much wood they had gathered from falling timber and some stones with sharp edges along with some kindling, moss, pine needles, and leaves. Most of the wood was wet due to the rain, but they did find a little that wasn't wet. They would use what dry wood they did find along with the animal dung back in the cave to dry out the wet wood. Once back in the cave things looked different; there were no more animal bones or plant debris. Michael and Hank were very impressed at Keith's cleaning jog as they came in he had been using a small bush to sweep out the cave. The animal dung and small bushes were in a neat little pile just outside the cave. They brought the items in Keith helped them to stack what they had collected against the inside of the cave wall. The girls were glad to see the boys were back looking forward to a warm fire. Hank and Michael would have to rely on their boy scout training to stay alive, and make it out of this mess alive. The fireman ship course taught them how to make a fire, how to extinguish a fire properly, and fire safety. Learning fireman ship was a must if you were going to build a fire in the boy scouts.

"What are the rocks for? We can't burn rocks?" Keith asked and the girls were also curious as to why. Michael and Hank laughed.

"Your right we can't burn the rocks. We brought back rocks for a couple of reasons," Michael explained as him and Hank was putting the rocks in a circle.

"We put the rocks in the circle like you see us doing here and build the fire in the center of the circle. When the rocks heat up they will reflect and help maintain heat, and we'll be making some tools from the rocks that will be helpful to us to use."

"Like what?" Keith asked. Both Amanda and Mae found this to be interesting.

"We'll be making a couple of knives and maybe an ax. No telling how long we may be here before we're found so we need to prepare, and pretty soon we will have to cut our own wood only so much can be found on the ground, "answered Michael.

"Whoa! What a cotton picking minute? You guys talk like we're going to be out here in this God forsaken woods for a long time. Maybe we should keep moving; maybe help is on the way. Besides, those mosquitoes are making a meal of me. Your going to look over here at me in a minute and see a skeleton," Keith said while scratching with one hand and swatting with the other.

"Listen Keith, everyone is tired and mosquito bitten, but we all need to keep in mind predators mostly come out at night and I don't have to tell you that man eating predators are in this area. Help may not come for days; no one knows where we are, we have a bunch we all are dealing with right now. We are on our own and like it or not we are all we have out here. It's no secret that our chances are slim, but chance also favors the prepared so we must do what we must to survive. Things will look better tomorrow for now let's just get through the night," said Michael.

"And I'm sure we all can agree on one thing, we need protection, warmth, and smoke from the fire will take care of the mosquitoes," Hank added.

"Mae and I were talking when you guys went for wood. It's probably a good idea to start showing the rest of us survival techniques; that was a scary thing when we all split up," said Amanda with concern.

"Yeah, school us on some things to better our chances," Mae added. Keith raised his hand to get everyone's attention saying, "an ax huh? Maybe there is something to this Boy Scout crap. I'm in too." Him saying that made them all smile. Michael and Hank also agreed this would increase their chances and then took turns explaining to them outdoor survival 101. The scouts picked up two rocks a piece and started to slowly tap them together, chipping small pieces from the other explaining to the rest as they worked, this technique was commonly known as knapping; to shape by breaking off pieces. The boys thrust for knowledge of the outdoors made them excel when it came to outdoor training. Michael's dad also showed Michael and Hank ways to survive in the wilderness the many times they had camped together. The scouts went on explaining how they all must work with what God made available with nature around them so being without any matches, lighters, or anything to make combustion they would attempt to make fire from friction. By the time they finished explaining about friction fire the boys were done making the stone knives. The two knives looked like something an explorer would find on an archaeological dig of a cave man's dwelling. The knives were small from handle to tip, averaging about eight to ten inches long. Three parts would be needed to make this fire work. One of the scouts took a small branch and started to furrow it out with his stone knife, making a long narrow trench down the middle of the branch, this made one. The second part to this was the kindling. A palm sized bird's nest was made from dried leaves and moss. This will be on stand-by so small sparks that make the amber which in turn will ignite dry materials. Once the branch with the narrow trench down the middle was made by Hank he laid it on the cave's floor placing he had whittled to a round-end, and this was the third part. Hank placed a small amount of dried leaves and moss within the trench and then put the rounded end in the narrow trench pushing down rubbing vigorously within four inches back and forth determined to build a fire from the friction. The fire making device proved to be a challenge; Hank and Michael took turns pushing and pulling the rounded stick down the wooden trench. Patience had to become your friend out in the wild if you wanted to come out alive. You could spend hours working on or making something and it still may not work. The scouts had to remind themselves that keeping your head while managing frustration was a must. The sun had gone down; the cave was so dark you could barely see your hand in front of your face. It was dark, cold, and everyone was hungry; things seemed hopeless. The darkness gave the cave an uneasy feeling. The crickets were loud outside doing their mating calls; the only other sound was the wood being rubbed together the boys worked staying at it not giving up. The moon and stars were out giving way to dim lighting outside with clear skies and a mild cool breeze that brought a chill to the night. Finally, slight hint of burning wood was the smell in the air they all was waiting for. A tiny amber came to life that tiny amber was the focus of everyone's attention. It seemed to be so bright in the darkness of the cave. They needed it to live so they in not to turn could live. The amber was transferred to the bird's nest kindling and the kindling to the wood that was in the rock circle. After being blown on a few times the fire caught on and grew bigger, lighting up the cave. The heat from the flames could be felt throughout the cave. Everyone's face could be seen with a smile, even Keith's. Michael and Hank gave each other a fist bump and they all circled around the fire. Mr. Wilson was still unconscious near the back of the cave's wall. They rejoiced knowing that the cold wouldn't be a problem tonight. The fire had a way of lifting morale; not only did it provide warmth, but also protection. Animals had the God given sense not to walk through fire. This fire was built inside the mouth of the cave leaving just enough room to walk by if they needed to get out. The animal dung was also placed in the fire to help dry the wet wood that was around the fire. Pine needles and leaves were spread about the cave's floor and everyone sat around the fire. Amanda was next to Michael, Mae was next to Hank, and Keith was closest to Wilson in their small circle. Wet leaves were put on the fire to make more smoke; this helped to run the mosquitoes out the cave. Some more wood was placed on the fire; no one was getting bit by mosquitoes anymore and was in their own thoughts winding down for the evening until they heard what sounded like a scuffle outside the cave. The loose gravel had given way to someone or something approaching the cave; someone or something had failed in their attempt to make up to where they were. Gravel could be heard being displaced as what or whoever was sliding back down the mountainside. The sound startled the group causing them to be frightened of this unknown. Michael and Hank stood grabbing their stone knives from their waist bands slowly walking outside the cave knives at the ready to deal with the threat.

Chapter 5

Cautiously, both scouts peered out into the night trying to adjust their eyes to the darkness below. It was evident they were at a disadvantage with the mouth of the cave being lit up by the fire making it harder for them to see into the night; giving sight advantage to whoever was below in the dark probably looking at them in the fire's light. The disadvantage was shared to whoever or whatever had fallen down the steep climb losing the surprise advantage. It was too dark to try navigating up or down this treacherous elevation. The fall from this high probably wouldn't kill you unless you fell on your head, but it could definitely break some bones.

"Michael, Hank, is that you guys up there?" 'A familiar voice came from below. Both scouts looked at each other.

"Who the heck are you lady?" Hank asked.

"It's me Beth, Van is down here too. The wolves split us up remember we were part of the group?"

"Yeah, we remember, but you set it off when you ran; instinctually animals will want to chase you. Was that you we heard fall?"

"No, that was Van he's laying flat on his back."

"I'm okay just got the wind knocked out of me," Van interjected feeling embarrassed.

"How can we get up there to that warm fire with you guys?" Beth said we'll come show you the way up.

"Could you hurry? We are so cold, tired, and these mosquitoes has made a meal out of use," pleaded Beth.

"Hang in there; we're moving fast as we can."

Everyone in the cave heard what was going on. Michael and Hank went back into the cave and made torches. They tore some more fabric from their clothing and wrapped it around some branches that were piled up for firewood then put fire to it. After carefully managing to make it down to where they were the scouts carefully guided Beth and Van up to the inside of the cave where they threw the torches into the fire. The girls all hugged and Van shook hands with Michael and Hank when he tried to shake with Keith, but Keith just stared into the fire.

"What happen to him?" Van asked pointing to Mr. Wilson who was laid out still unconscious.

"He's been that way for some time. We keep checking his pulse making sure he's alive. It is our belief that he has a concussion," answered Mae. They took the time to catch each other up on the past events that happened since they separated.

"Beth and I were wondering about aimlessly until we heard what sounded like a scream. We weren't going to go at first being scared to walk like a scream. We wasn't going to go at first being scared to walk in this direction of the scream because it might have been a wolf or some other danger causing someone to scream out like that, but we agreed to take a chance anyway. Then we saw this fire; it could be seen from a ways out; that's what led us here," said Van.

"I'm sure the scream you heard was me; when Michael reset my arm it hurt worse than anything I've ever felt. A couple of good things came out of it; I have the use of my arm again and indirectly it led you guys back to us," Hank mused. The fire looked and felt good especially to Beth and Van as they sat there with the others welcoming the heat and to be away from those blood thirsty mosquitoes. The smoke from the fire had run them away and kept out of the cave. Van had been cradling his hand the whole time.

"Hey, do you guys think you could do something with my hand?" Van says as he holds up his right hand. It was obvious some of his fingers were broken; two of them were in positions fingers shouldn't be and swollen. The fingers had to be set or Van ran the risk of losing his hand. He was told to lie down on his back; his shoe laces were removed. Michael prepared some small sticks to be tied to Van's fingers in order to hold them straight and grow back in place in time, and he was given one to bite down on when the pain came. Everyone was asked to hold him down. It was good everyone was holding Van because he bucked and screamed the whole time from the intense pain. They felt bad for him, but it was a necessary evil. Michael and Hank were doing the resetting while Mae and Amanda did the wrapping. Van was sweating profusely by the time they got to the last finger and then he passed out from the pain. They knew he was alive because he was still breathing kind of hard. It had been a challenging day for them all; they were physically and mentally tired rest was desperately needed. The girls cuddled together while the boys and Wilson was off to the side. Sleep was welcomed as it overcame them all. Hours later the sun began to rise with the dew glistening off of the plants from the rays of our closest star. Birds were singing their morning songs; insects were bathing and drinking in the moisture. Critters were scurrying about in search of food and becoming food to those who ate them. Pine and flowers could be smelt as the group started to awake to a fire that saved their life last night, but now it barely existed. Some faint coals were left quickly dying out. Michael put more wood on the coals and got down to ground level blowing the heated wood back to life and flames danced around the wood.

"We must be careful not to let this fire ever go out. Let me put it another way; if this fire dies we die," said

Hank standing and pointing at their campfire. Michael decided to put stronger meaning to what Hank was saying," which meant gathering some more wood and saving the big log pieces to burn through the night. Besides, I was thinking of what Van said last night about this fire could be seen a good ways out. This can work for us, which means it increases our chances of being seen for rescue."

"Yeah, that's all good and dandy, but a fire can only be seen real good at night. Again we all need to go back to the bus where they will be looking for us while it's daytime," said Keith.

"Keith, the way we survive is to work together; why must you always be in opposition?" Michael asked.

"Because this whole situation sucks and I can't sit around here and die."

"No one wants to die here, back at the bus, or anywhere else for that matter. We can put all of our heads together and talk about rescue, but for the moment there are more pressing matters that need our attention first," said Michael with urgency in his voice.

"Oh yeah like what?"

"Restroom breaks!" Amanda said. It was obvious with everyone just waking up; it would stand to reason that relief was needed.

"I don't think anyone should be alone with wild animals around," said Mae.

"Agreed, when anyone goes we should always have someone nearby in case of danger. Does anyone disagree?" Hank asked and no one disagreed. Van raised his hand to speak as if he was still in a classroom.

"Would you spit it out man? We ain't in no damn schoolroom and don't have no time for your bull crap you book heads make a guy turn bully," yelled Keith.

"Hey! Let's all calm down. Keith we all must have a say. Go ahead Van speak your mind," said Michael still looking at Keith who was now standing with him. Van pointed to the unconscious Wilson and said, "what about him? How do we know when it's time for him to go relieve himself?" There was a long pause; no one had given thought to that.

"We won't until we smell it!" Keith answered. They all went to relieve themselves and were now making it back to the cave. Once inside they all took in the sights looking out from this elevated position gave them a much better view. Nothing could be seen for miles around, but the treetops canvassing the entire area as far as the eyes could see and another mountain a good distance away. Was this the mountain they tumbled down? The sight was so beautiful everyone was silent taking in the beauty and from what they learned in a short time of being here also deadly. Beth broke the silence, "am I the only one that's thirsty and hungry?" Everyone, but Keith admitted to being hungry.

"How in the hell can all of you be hungry at a time like this? Let me bring you slow boys and girls up on our current situation. First, let's start with what I'd like to call sequence of events. We are hundreds of miles from civilization and we don't even know what state we are in. Let's not forget the monster mudslide that caused our accident killing most of the people that came with us on this trip. Then we all had to run for our lives from that vicious pack of wolves. Then the mosquitoes were out for our blood; then the temperature dropped and almost froze our rear ends off which brings us to this point. Yes, I'm thirsty and hungry like the rest of you, but I'm not into living like animals in a cave. We must go wait at the bus for help while its daylight," Keith said with seriousness in his voice.

"Keith, this may come as a surprise to you but, I agree with you. We do need to go back to the bus," agreed Michael. Hank and the rest of the group had looks on their faces like they couldn't believe Michael agreed to go back to the bus where they all knew had a strong wolf presence.

"Finally, you've come to your senses; come on let's go," said Keith in a hurry to leave the cave.

"Hold on big fellow, only a few of us should go, and only to bring back the things we need for our survival. We are in a serious and deadly situation so any and all of our decisions affect the whole group; we are in survival mode. Beth your right we need food and water if we are to survive this and be rescued." Keith started to say something in protest to what Michael just said, but Michael continued to talk not giving him a chance.

"Hank, what should a person or persons do when stranded out in the great outdoors with lives at stake?" Hank knew this stuff as second nature.

"First, find shelter, than if possible make a fire. The fire isn't just for warmth, but also protection, and it builds up morale giving you hope; then food and water depending on your situation. Sometimes the food and water can come before the fire, but water should be boiled, and the meat should be cooked to be safe. There is a good chance any water we drink out here will be from a stream or river. We must kill any harmful bacteria or parasites; those nasty little microorganisms can make you very sick with the Hershey squirts and unchecked you could die. So again fire plays a very important part in survival."

"What's Hershey squirts?" Beth asked.

"Diarrhea!" Keith answered loudly.

"That's not so bad; doesn't that clean you out?" She asked.

"Yeah, but it dehydrates your body and we are in need of water. Diahhrea would drain the body of fluids," Hank explained. Keith tried making his point again.

"Us standing around planning and talking about body waste is a bunch of hog wash and pigeon puddle. That still doesn't change the fact that none of us have any idea where we are not to mention what state we're in. We should be heading for the bus right now."

"Not knowing where we are is not entirely true. I don't know our exact location, but I did notice what state we're in. I saw the Wyoming sign when we crossed over the state line coming from Colorado on highway 25. We passed a town when we entered this state some hours ago called Cheyenne; that's when the bus driver got off the main route and took some back roads. The first road we took was to the left; then another turn to the right, then another right, and the last road we took was on the left which led to the mountain we came crashing down," added Van.

"Van, I was on the same bus as you and I don't remember all of that," Hank disclosed. No one else remembered that to such detail either.

"I guess you could say that memory is my strong point. I have a photographic memory; anything I see I can remember in detail and my favorite subject is history; history of the United States."

"Oh, wow that's just what we need; a guy who remembers history. We don't solve problems out here with pen and paper boy. There are two kinds of people in this world; those who talk about what they are going to do and those who do what they are going to do so let's do something," Keith commented.

"Any and all information can be useful at this point. Van what can you tell us about this state Wyoming?" Michael asked.

"Well let's see; Wyoming has the lowest population of all the states, but is the ninth largest state in square miles. Only Alaska has a lower population density; Wyoming is like the open space." Before Van could finish Keith interrupted.

"What are you some kind of nerdish geek? Who remembers crap like that?"

"Keith the rest of us would like to hear what he has to say. Is that alright by you?" Michael asked.

"By all means waste what daylight we have. I'm on the edge of my seat to hear the rest of this crap; by all means go on Van," said Keith sarcastically.

"Keith, do you have to be so abrasive with your tone?" Van asked nervously.

"Spit it out!" Keith yelled balling both fists up.

"Okay, where was I? Oh yeah, Wyoming; the sheep and cattle outnumber the people in this state by more than a five to one ratio. Wyoming has many coal mines; the Black Thunder Coal Mine in Wright is the largest in the country. Mountain men in search of beaver pelts were the first to explore the state in the early nineteenth century. Men such as Kit Carson, Jedediah Smith, and Jim Bridger roamed the area. Yellowstone was designated the first national park in 1872. Too bad we never made it there," Van said hanging his head. The way Van retained information was jaw dropping; that's how he kept good grades. Reluctantly, Keith saw how food and water would benefit them to keep up their strength and stay alive so the plan was to get food, water, and if there was enough daylight left go to the bus. Beth and Van would remain behind with Mr. Wilson while the rest would do the searching. Hank, Keith, Michael, Mae, and Amanda checked the base of the mountain staying within the sound of each other's voice. The sun was shining bright being at its apex and giving the plant life the photosynthesis they need by which the cells in green plants convert sunlight to chemical energy. At the same time warming the earth; the traveling five was hot and very thirsty and hunger was also a problem. So far water was nowhere to be found. However, they did happen to come across a small game trail. The group stopped as Hank took a closer inspection.

"Looks to be rabbit tracks along with some kind of rodent tracks; I'm not sure what kind of rodent," Hank explained.

"We could set some snares along the way and hopefully catch something to eat before nightfall," Michael suggested.

"Okay, let's do it," Hank agreed.

"What's a snare?" Amanda asked.

"Hunters use them to trap like a noose used for capturing small animals."

"Which begs the questions, what can we use to make a snare out of?" Mae asked.

"Anything we can tie off alone this trail that serves to entangle what we can eat. Maybe like a vine or something," answered Michael. Mae had an idea, "how about my shoe strings?" She suggested.

"Yeah, shoestrings would work." Michael and Hank set four traps ten yards apart from the other and went on searching for water. The group went a little farther around the mountain and then heard it and after going down about another hundred yards through the trees and brush they saw a raging river with rapids. The current appeared too strong to cross on foot. The sun was gleaming off the water which never looked so good to thirsty individuals who moments ago didn't know where their next drink would come from. They all had made it down from their elevation to flat ground and was fifty yards away from the river when Keith broke from the group running towards the river.

"Keith no!" Michael yelled as he took off in a run after him. The girls didn't know what was going on, but they ran behind Hank; Keith was close to the river now.

"Keith don't drink the water yet!" shouted Michael on the run to him. Keith had made it to the river bank dropping to his knees to bend forward and drink from the river when he was plowed into causing him to roll along the side of the bank of the river.

Chapter 6

Michael had used all of his might slamming into
Keith, but Keith recovered and got to his feet before
Michael. He bent down grabbing Michael by his collar
helping him to his feet only to punch Michael in his face
knocking him down, Keith turned to meet Hank's fist to his
jaw that sent him on his back hard. Keith was quick when
he kicked out causing Hank's legs to slide out from under
him; he lost his balance and hit the ground. Keith tried
standing, but Michael was on him; they rolled about the
ground with each man trying to throw a punch and gain top
control. Keith knew how to use his weight when he shifted
which was now on top only to be handled by Hank who
was being aided by Michael. Keith was barely being
restrained by both of the scouts; he was hard to hold down.
Amanda and Mae arrived to see Keith thrashing wildly.

"Keith…the water… isn't safe to…drink yet!"
Michael said between breathes from being winded.

"Alright! The both of you... get your chicken...chockers... off me!" Reluctantly Michael and Hank released Keith not sure if he would try for a cheap shot, but they couldn't hold him down for long. All three men stood up breathing hard and wiping the dirt from their clothes.

"I'm thirsty and excited about finding water; I didn't think a small drink would hurt."

"Keith, don't you remember we all went over this water thing back at the cave; bactcria and parasitcs remember?" Amanda asked.

"Personally, if you want your body to be a host to some parasites and be a butthead about it; it's no skin off my bottom, but when it affects the rest of us you need to check yourself," Mae added.

"How would me getting sick or dying for that matter affect any of you? Huh, tell me?"

"Keith, you just don't get it. Whatever your disposition concerning others none of us want to see your or anyone get hurt or dead. Being ignorant getting hurt is acceptable because you couldn't know no better, but knowing better and still doing the wrong thing would be downright stupid. If anyone of us gets hurt we all would do what must to help. The unnecessary time we spend on something that could have been avoided is wasted on something we could have done on something to increase our chances to survive," said Mae.

"Mae's right you know we all came here together and since we are away from our families we are a family when it comes to our survival. We need to help each other and work together at getting out of this mess. None of us want to be here as you've said it sucks," Amanda said with a smile.

"Throughout my whole life especially when my mother died; my father is a work-a-holic. He works all the time and it's always been me taking care of me, always!"

"To survive this we need to work as one and stop all this fighting among each other. Everyone made a good point even you Keith," Michael paused to let his words sink in. All that could be heard was the moving water they stood by. Keith you don't have to go at it alone with us here with you. We should work and think as a pack," Michael explained.

"Yeah, well I know a little about animals so who is the leader? Who is the alpha of our so called pack cause I don't want to follow anyone. If I can't be the alpha damn this pack thing," Keith said loudly.

"Man your always crying about something. What are the babies gonna do if you keep doing all the crying?" Hank asked. The girls turned their heads holding back their laughter.

"I'll show you who will do the crying," said Keith walking towards Hank. Hank balled his fist up ready for the encounter when Michael stepped in between the two.

"Chill out the both of you!" Looking them both in their eyes they both backed away, then Michael went on to say, "Keith, in this pack we all can be the alphas."

"How can that be?" Keith asked.

"We all vote on difficult choices and the majority of the votes decide so how about it. Let's all be a super alpha pack?" Everyone, but Keith said, "yes."

"Keith will you allow me to show you something," asked Hank.

"Be my guess; you got the floor; what's on your mind?" Everyone even Michael was curious what Hank was doing when he went to a nearby tree and picked up a fallen branch and broke six medium width sticks from it, walked over to Keith, and handed him one. Keith looked at the stick in his hand and asked Hank," what do I do with this?" Hank wanted to tell him to shut up and wait, but knew in order for him to get through to Keith he would have to be tactful and more diplomatic.

"Keith, it's no secret that you are the strongest out of our pack. Let's see if you can break the stick I've given you." Keith breaks it with very little effort and says, "okay now what?" Hank takes the two broken pieces of stick from Keith and hands him the five remaining sticks.

"I just want to show you an illustration of us. The stick you broke was one person on their own. The five you hold in your hand now is you, Mae, Amanda, Michael, and me. Break the five if you can," and saying that made Keith want to break them even more so he tried. The sticks wouldn't break so now he gave it his all with an intense stare at what didn't give even with all of his might the five sticks wouldn't break. Keith threw the sticks aside somewhat frustrated and looked at Hank.

"You see us together is stronger than we would ever be apart," Hank said extending his hand to Keith who shook it.

"I guess I can roll with it; this pack thing as long as it's not a one man show. I give you my word we survive this thing together."

"Keith, this is not to take a jab at you, but how do we know that you will keep your word?" Michael asked. Keith looked as if he wanted to fight and then his features softened when he said, "because I gave my word and that's something I don't take lightly. A man without his word is a hollow man; my father always said." Michael extended his hand to Keith.

"That's good enough for me," said Michael. The rest of them ran and gave Keith a hug.

"Hey, I just had a thought; Van and Beth didn't get the chance to vote on the pack thing like the rest of us," mentioned Amanda.

"It wouldn't have mattered; we have the majority votes anyway," Keith said smiling for the first time.

"I have a question more to the point," said Mae looking at the moving water.

"How do we take some of that with us?" They directed their attention to the abundant amount of liquid that would keep them alive. They faced the painful fact that they would have to leave for now without a drop of water to taste or take with them due to not having anything to put it in. Most of their lips were dry and starting to crack due to loss of moisture. The scouts knew it took 3-4 days to die of dehydration. Michael and Hank were confident they wouldn't have to wait that long. On the way, Hank remembered something looking at the high grass to the shaded area; the sun was blocked out due to the trees. He removed his jacket and then his shirt; the group stopped to watch and see what he was doing. Michael caught on and started doing the same. When both men were down to their t-shirts and pants they put their jackets back on and ran through the high grass dragging their shirts collecting moisture on the fabric. Then went over by the others so they could see them squeeze their shirts overhead with mouths open, drops of water went down their arms, on their faces, and in their mouths. The dew from the morning hadn't dried up yet. The rest of the group didn't need to be told what to do with the thirst driving them so they followed suit and repeated the process over and over again. It wasn't enough to totally quench the thirst, but just enough to curve it. The girls had mentioned how they wish they had their purses they left on the bus with their lip gloss in them. At least now they knew where to find the water. They would come back with something to hold the water and take it back to camp to boil. Heading back to the cave they were fortunate to find the four traps that was set; two had caught rabbits. One of them was dead and the other was still alive trying to free itself from the snare. Michael moved fast to get to the struggling rabbit and broke its neck quickly so the animal wouldn't suffer. Everything was the same when they made it back to the cave. The girls told Van and Beth about the river and all of them being alphas in their little pack with say so and how to do the shirt thing to get some water. After Beth and Van did the shirt thing they went back to the cave and did what they could to squeeze some drops of water from their shirts in Mr. Wilson's mouth. Amanda and Mae had tried making him more comfortable by taking off their jackets using one for him a pillow and the other to partially cover him even though the cave was warmed by the fire.

Hank, Keith, and Michael were down at the foot of the mountain showing Keith how to skin the rabbits with their rock knives and how to clean them.

"Why couldn't we do this cleaning in or outside the cave the cave?" Keith asked.

"Well, you don't want the blood or fresh meat to attract predators where you lay our head. When it comes to blood, any gear or clothing that it gets on should be washed if possible, buried, or burned. That's why we are being careful not to get any blood on our clothing," Michael explained. Hank held up the two dressed out rabbits.

"Now we make a spit and cook these bad boys."

"Hold on, your telling me we spit on these rabbits before we cook them?" Keith asked scratching his head."

"No, what Hank means is cut, slender pointed rod then we run it through the meat to cook over an open fire. It's the pointed rod the meat is on that's called a spit," Michael added. Keith had finally come around to wanting to learn; surviving was a big motivation.

"Maybe there is something to this outdoor Boy Scout stuff you guys have learned." The cooked rabbits gave off a good, grilled aroma throughout the cave. The cooked fat from the rabbits were used to put on their chapped lips. These rabbits had very little fat, but it helped their lips from being dry and also had a soothing effect. Everyone was hungry and thirsty, but the smell of cooked food made the hunger outweigh the thirst. The licking of fingers was a testament to the meat tasting good. This high protein meat revived the whole group. They sat around the fire developing a plan of action, but didn't forget to check on Wilson from time to time. His lips were dry and beginning to crack like most of the group so animal fat was applied to his too. Hank and Keith would make the trip back to the bus with hopes of a search party at the bus or nearby looking for them; if not then get the supplies they could to better their survival out in this wilderness. Seven long poles were cut and then they sharpened the ends making spears for longer reach in case of danger. Then fire hardened the tips by letting the flames burn them just a little by rolling them around top of the fire. The three headed out with their spears and rock knives leaving Beth,

Amanda, Mae, and Van a spear a place. Although, they probably would never use them it gave a small degree of comfort knowing that you could defend yourself with something. It was shortly after noon so they would need to move in a hurry while it was still daylight. Unless it was a must trying to navigate this terrain in the dark would be an idiot's move. Someone could take a fall a good ways down; break a leg stepping into a hole or become dinner for a predator.

"How do you guys know we're going in the right direction?" Keith asked.

"On the way here we watched for landmarks," said Michael as each man walked in single file using their spears for walking canes.

"Landmarks, what do you mean?"

"Well, you look for identifying features of a landscape. Things you know won't move, stuff like mountains, large rocks, trees, hills, and so on," Michael said pointing around them.

"Trees! They all look the same, and most with the same color."

"Keith out here most plants and wildlife has adapted to fit in with their surroundings. Although, color is a factor look more for shape. If you really take a closer look at the trees they have different shapes." Taking a closer look at the trees, they noticed the branches and tree trunks looked different. A new world opened up to Keith making him more observant than ever before. Now instead of just looking for color, but more so shapes it was truly fascinating all of this life around him in his past he paid little or no attention to. The three had traveled out of the grasslands being very aware of their surroundings danger could come without warning fast. They soon found out that this state was abundant with wildlife. Off to a distance they saw elk, buffalo, and antelope. To down one of these would mean good eating for a while, but it was next to impossible with the weapons they had. The three went a little farther and was shocked to hear a sound like rolling thunder as a herd of wild horses came galloping by far off the ground sounded loud. Hank wanted Keith to be brought up to speed on the great outdoors as much as possible. They kept moving when he said, "wolves ain't the only predators that we need to watch for; be on the lookout for bear, panther, wild boar, badger, wolverine, or any animal that has their young nearby. They will attack to protect thinking their young are in danger. Don't take anything for granite; every animal and everything of nature has a purpose and is hardwired to survive which means they will defend themselves to the death and will kill if they feel they need to. Oh and keep in mind out here we're still in their house so the best thing to do is to be good house guests even though we are uninvited. The three traveled farther in silence taking in the layout of the land; so far there was no sign of civilization for miles around. There was land and more land, meadows, valleys, and mountains could be seen from elevated positions as they walked nearing the bus wreckage and still no sign of civilization. There the bus sat slightly tipped against this big tree with hardened mud and encasing the wheels. The sight looked less menacing in the daylight until the three went aboard and see what was left of the bodies. Clearly, animals had been feasting on the human remains. The smell and the sight were horrible. What once was human beings were now twisted and broken skeletons; some still in their seats. After a long moment the young men came to the realization that time was against them and knew they must move fast or the same fate would befall them. This morbid, disgusting sight caused the young men to reflect back to when they were the ones who were able to walk away from this awful accident; they were in those same seats yesterday when everyone was alive; what a difference a day made. The three were brought back to the present abruptly with the sounds of two birds fighting on the bus not even six feet from them. The birds were fighting over something that had their full attention, flapping their wings, pecking with their beaks, and feathers were flying. It became apparent they were at war over someone's eyeball. The three moved along the isle waving their arms scaring away the birds that had gotten in through the door and broken windows. Being careful not to step on any grisly remains each went to where they were seated grabbing their backpacks. Some were still on the overhead racks; others were tossed about the bus. The young men then went on to the front of the bus grabbing all the food the animals didn't get to storing it in their backpacks along with the first kid kit, some road flares, a fire extinguisher, and all the bottles of water they could find along with whatever cell phones they could collect and a flashlight. Before leaving Michael and Hank went into their backpacks and put their knives on their sides no longer needing the stone knives. Michael and Hank gave them to Keith who liked the feel of the knives in his hands. He put them both in his waistband at the small of his back. On the way out Keith grabbed someone's guitar, put his arm through the strap, and swung it around to his back over his backpack. As they exited the bus, Keith got stuck trying to get out. The neck of the guitar was protruding just above his head. He had to stoop down to clear the doorway. Once outside the young men picked up their spears they had leaned against the bus and were on the way back to camp.

"Can you play that thing?" Hank asked pointing at the guitar strapped to Keith's back.

"Yeah I been playing since I was knee high to a dog. Not much for singing though; every time I try to sing and think I'm singing good, but it don't come out right or so I've been told. I figured maybe some music would lighten the mood from time to time."

It was Keith's turn to ask a question. "I got to ask, what made you get the fire extinguisher? We won't be putting out any fires will we?" Keith questioned.

"Let's hope it won't come to that, but you never know; we will find some use for it. I was always told that it is better to have and not need then to need and not have," answered Hank.

The sun was beginning to get low in the sky so they were traveling faster back to the camp. Taking a break long enough to drink a bottle of water a piece leaving seventeen bottles of water to ration among the group and now they had means to boil water from the river that was just around the mountain from their camp. For the most part the young men felt good accomplishing their goal getting important supplies that would be paramount to their well-being. Getting back on the move along the way was talk about how disappointed everyone would be once they found out there wasn't any search party at the crash site waiting on them. They would have to survive this on their own without outside help. Keith was doing better with his bearings; he knew which way to go in case they got separated. Hank and Michael had drilled it into his head that the sun shined in their cave during sunset and the sun was now at their back so they needed to head back due east because the sun rises in the east and sets in the west. Traveling to the bus they were facing the sun; returning to the cave the sun needed to be at their backs. Keith felt comfortable and more secure knowing these things as he walked behind the scouts. He was a person use to being in control and this outdoor thing was new to him, but it seemed as if he was beginning to like it. The scouts were teaching him the ways of the wild, ways to be in control out here; he couldn't help, but to take in things were interesting. Not knowing eyes were watching them; a hungry panther was stalking them from high ground, and had been for some time. No one was aware of the immediate danger. The panther took a running leap with his eyes on the neck of the last man walking in

the single file line bearing his teeth and claws for the kill.

Chapter 7

The sun was beginning to give way to night; it was that time of evening just before night, dusk. Mae and Amanda were sitting at the mouth of the cave with their legs hanging over the edge looking about this beautiful country from above with hopes of seeing the fellows leading the search party to help get them all back home safe and sound.

"They should have been back already," said Amanda.

"Yeah I was thinking the same thing. What do you think is keeping them?" Mae asked.

"No way of knowing for now, we may have to go after them."

"Let's not talk like that Amanda. I refuse to believe anything negative, I've been praying for their safe return."

"Maybe they're on their way as we speak," said Beth walking up behind them taking a seat between the two.

"I have an interesting question that just caught my eye as I walked up, what is that over there?" Beth asked pointing to their left. Amanda and Mae didn't see it at first, than off in a distance for a brief moment there was Van to witness what they had seen. When he came the girls were pointing, but there was nothing to see, but wide open space of the great outdoors.

"What am I suppose to be looking for?" Van asked.

The girls were still looking waiting with hopes of the twinkle to happen again so Van could see what they had seen.

"It was something shining a long ways off, but none of us can make out what it was," Beth explained.

"We may not know what it was, but I can tell you what it wasn't. Whatever it was it had to be manmade to give off light or to reflect light the way it did," Mae reasoned.

"What if it was the guys trying to signal us for help?" Amanda asked.

"Let's say for the sake of arguments that it was them out there, no way are any of us going out there in the dark. Besides, I'm sure them guys can take care of themselves and wouldn't want us out there exposed with no daylight," Van said with authority.

"No doubt in my mind that you are right and I know the best thing to do is to be patient and wait here for their return, but I don't have to like it." Amanda responded standing to go back into the cave, when they heard a growl below them. The growl was so loud and deep it scared everyone into quickly standing to their feet they looked down to see what it was. From the limited light it appeared some animal was on his way to come up to where they were. It was something big and hairy that moved about huffing and breathing hard; a bear!

*

Michael and Hank heard the thud, but Keith felt the blow to his back. Everyone was taken by surprise; Keith fell to the ground face first dropping his spear. Not knowing it at the time, but by strapping the guitar to his back inadvertently saved his life. The panther had mistaken the neck of the guitar for Keith's back; it had bitten into the stringed instrument. This didn't discourage the big cat as it shook side to side with its powerful jaws clamped on the guitar and the claws stayed locked on Keith's back; he winced from the prick of the claws. The panther bit for its prey's neck again only splintering the wood the guitar was made of. Hank and Michael went into action fast yelling and poking at the big cat with their spears. The panther hissed showing his menacing curved teeth, while still on Keith's back holding him down not wanting to give up its meal. Slowly the four legged terror moved to the side when Michael and Hank continued poking at it with their spears. This feline began to charge from time to time swatting its sharp claws at Hank and Michael then taking a few steps back hissing and growling. Keith was now up on his fast grabbing his fallen spear and charged for the big cat, stabbing it in the left side, but Keith's trust wasn't hard enough to pierce the tough hide of this animal. The panther was quick, after being poked from Keith it turned taking a swipe at him. The blow caught Keith in the forearm ripping through his jacket causing him to back up some. There was very little light left and the movements of the panther were so swift no one could seem to get a good stab into its hide. The scouts kept trying, they knew if they let this man eater run off the chances would be high it would stalk out and hunt them later picking them off as prey one by one. That chance was too great; they must do what they must to put this predator down for good. Michael seen an opening and went for it thrusting a bit too low overextending his reach

and paid for it when the panther dug four shallow lines

across his cheek. Small blood droplets could be seen, but

this allowed Hank and Keith to move in. Hank's spear

penetrated between the animal's rib cage which caused it to

shift and expose it's soft under belly. Hank held it in that

position long enough for Keith to take full advantage

stabbing repeatedly in the stomach, Michael joined in to

finish the panther off. The big cat lay still and the three

stopped stabbing, but kept their spears in the panther. All

they could hear was each other breathing, sucking in big

gulps of air not even the crickets made a sound. The three

looked at each other; Hank held his spear high in one hand

and gave a shout of joy. Michael and Keith held their spear

high and did the same. Then the three returned to the cave;

they noticed the fire was built high and burning bright at

the cave's entrance. As they neared the heat from the

flames were very intense. Keith, Hank, and Michael

entered the cave being ever so cautious not to get burnt. To their surprise everyone except Wilson was standing close together with spears pointing at them; sweat was dripping from their faces and their eyes were wide with fear.

Chapter 8

Amanda, Mae, Beth, and Van told them how they heard and seen the bear coming up to the cave so everyone retreated back into the cave and began throwing wood on the fire building it higher and grabbed their spears, hoping and praying the big bear wouldn't come in. The fire must have discouraged it.

"Then about an hour later you guys came in," said Van. When it was Michael, Hank, and Keith's turn they told them about the trip to the bus while giving everyone a bottle of water. They informed them that there was no search party, but they were able to bring back supplies, and about the attack of the panther. That's when a serious look came over Keith's face, and he spoke loud enough for everyone to hear.

"I never told you two thanks for saving my life back there when that panther had me down. I'm alive this moment to tell the rest of you that this sticking together pack thing works." They all came together embracing with a group hug.

"We had to kill the big cat before it killed us. Shame we put too many holes in it because we probably could have used his hide for a rug or something," added Keith. This brought laughter to the cave with Keith joining in too. The scouts used the first aid kit to treat and bandage Keith and Michael's wounds the big cat had inflicted. Mr. Wilson finally awakened and they informed him where they were and their situation. Wilson was weak, hungry, and thirsty. Everyone sat and ate the food that was prepared for the trip they had retrieved from the cooler that was on the bus, all the provisions inside was still intact. The food had to be rationed because there wasn't much of it; maybe this food could be stretched for a couple of days. The water could be drunk at will due to the abundance of it around side of the mountain with the flowing river; it just had to be boiled. Once Wilson ate and had his fill of water the scouts helped him to walk outside and gave him some privacy leaning him against the rocky mountain as they turned their backs so Wilson could relieve himself. When they returned to the cave he laid down and fell into a deep sleep again. His body was too week and still healing from being injured in the crash. Everyone was glad; it appeared Wilson would make it. The next couple of days went by without incident. Wilson was in and out of sleep; some of the times mumbling still unconscious. The pack continued to monitor him from time to time. Staying busy and keeping each other in good spirits while trying to formulate a plan to self-rescue since being rescued by any outside help seemed more like a fairytale as the days went by. The good news was that the bear hadn't returned, but the pack remained cautious and watchful, especially at night; that's when they kept the fire high. The scouts showed the pack how to boil water in a plastic bottle. Mae, Amanda, Beth, Keith, and Van couldn't reason how anyone could boil water in a plastic bottle, it defied their logic. Hank and Michael showed them by taking one of the full bottles of water and tying a shoestring to the neck of the bottle, than tied the string to a stick. All eyes were watching as the scouts removed the cap from the bottle and extended the bottle just above the flames.

"This is where the fire is the hottest," the scouts explained.

"The idea is not to let the flames touch the plastic, there will be a little shrinkage, but no real damage to the bottle. Bringing it to a boil for several seconds should be enough to kill germs or parasites." It was hard to believe their eyes; the four became believers when the water began to boil in the plastic bottle without the plastic melting. All the food that was salvaged from the bus was gone; snaring a few rabbits, squirrels, and finding edible plants to eat here and there was a blessing to their survival. Evening was setting in with everyone sitting around the fire talking.

"I was wondering, boiling water to drink, keeping the fire alive, not knowing when we will catch our next meal or what roots to eat and constantly living around danger. How long do you all think we can keep this up? Beth asked.

"Beth we all are just doing our best to survive," answered Amanda.

"Yeah I know and I'm not complaining or putting any one down. If it wasn't for Michael and Hank's outdoor training I'm sure I'd be somewhere hurt or worse somewhere dead. I was just wondering what's our end game," reasoned Beth.

The cave became silent for several seconds as everyone gave thought to her words. The only sounds at that moment were the crackling of the fire and the crickets outside doing their mating calls.

"She has a good point. I know we've went over several what if's, but no real plan of action. What about suggestions? Does anyone have anymore suggestions?" Van asked.

"I'm ready for whatever. I'm not the only one starting to get cabin fever being cooped up in this cave am I?" Keith asked.

"I'm in agreement, we have gotten a bit too content just being here," added Michael.

"Okay since everyone including myself is getting antsy let's start preparing to make a move. There has to be some sort of light at the end of the tunnel," suggested Hank.

"Oh yeah light!" Van exclaimed. Keith looked at Hank, than at Michael before asking, "what on earth is he talking about?"

"Before you guys returned from the bus we girls saw a light or reflection out there in a far off distance. When we called Van to see it, it was no longer there." Amanda answered.

"I guess with the bear scare and the absence of you guys, the light we seen slipped our minds," Mae added apologetically. When they went outside the cave it was well into the evening. The sun had set, there was an easterly wind making known the likelihood of rain was without question. The girls were showing the rest of the group which direction they seen this light. At the present no one saw any evidence of light or anything resembling a light source. Michael and Hank knew the way they were pointing was west.

"Tomorrow a few of us could scout several miles in that direction, see what we can find, "said Michael.

"Me and Mae would like to go with you guys this time, "said Amanda. This was Mae's first time hearing of this, but Amanda was her girl and she would side with her. They needed to stretch their legs anyway. Before Michael could object to them coming along everyone was startled with the surprise of a deep-throated growl. Their attention was torn from staring across the horizon. No one noticed or heard the bear creeping up the mountain from the forest; it was too close for comfort. No one had to be told to get back into the cave. Once there, they attempted to build the fire higher with hopes of it warding off the monster, only to find that no one stocked up the wood pile for this night so their hopes dropped. Michael and Hank mentally beat themselves up for allowing something this important to go unattended. History had proven people had died for less. All had gone to the back of the cave arming themselves with spears. Wilson was starting to stir around behind them. The fire was still lit, but it was only glowing reddish-orange coals, roaring flames would be needed to discourage this bear. It could casually walk around this fire to get to them with no problem, the same way they had walked around it. Everyone watched the mouth of the cave waiting to see this brute being very anxious, fear gripped them, and sweat could be seen on their faces. Although, it knew how to navigate this terrain the loose gravel told every step this creature took. Another growl, it was closer and had to be right at the entrance of the cave, but it couldn't be seen, and then came silence. They couldn't hear the bear only their breathing. The anticipation could be seen on the group faces by the fire light; the reality was the claws alone from an animal of this size and its strength could do great bodily injury or rip you to shreds. Wilson had awakened, stood from his travois and stretched while asking, "what's up with the big sticks in everyone's hands?"

"Shhh… A big bear is out there," said Hank never taking his eyes off the mouth of the cave. The group looked on in horror as Wilson grabbed Beth's spear from her hands, bumped his way past in front of them walking to the mouth of the cave.

"Mr. Wilson, no," Michael said in a low voice.

"You kids stay back, I got this."

Chapter 9

The thoughts that went through Wilson's head compelled him to be the protector of these children. He was amazed and proud how far these kids had gotten, the shelter, the food, and the water they had somehow provided it all. Even when saving his life, when they could have been selfish and left him to the wolves. The nerve of some stupid bear to test his resolve; he would not have no simple-minded bear standing in the way of their survival, not now, not ever. Wilson wasn't a brave man by any standard. Two failed marriages with two ex-wives who had taken almost all of his money and hadn't birthed any children, but somehow he felt like a father figure at this moment. Maybe it was instinctual. Paternal, a need to protect, something these teenagers wouldn't understand. Wilson was cautious and slowed his steps holding his spear with both hands in front of him, ready to do this animal some harm. Maybe it had left; Wilson began to think to himself. Suddenly, the massive brute appeared on all fours making its way a few feet inside the cave. Wilson went on the attack stabbing the beast with the spear just below the shoulder. The bear growled then stood and struck out at Wilson with its huge claws. The blow caught Wilson in his mid-section knocking the air from him. The force of the blow lifted Wilson from the ground as he went sailing into the cave's wall breaking many of his bones then falling to the cave's floor. The impact ended his life as he lay twisted up as a contortionist there at their feet. The girls screamed! At the same time Hank yelled, "nooo!" Then he ran at the standing bear; this brute struck out at Hank the same way it had Wilson. Hank was ready and ducked under the deadly claws then stabbed upwards into the beast throat, but wasn't fast enough to evade what came next. The bear back-handed Hank up off his feet; Hank landed on his back banging his head against the fire extinguisher knocking him unconscious. The monster looked at the rest of them spread his arms wide as if to say whose next? Roaring so loud it hurt the ears inside the cave. The whole pack witnessed what had happened to Wilson and Hank. All the fear they were experiencing now turned to anger and they collectively yelled back just as loud as the bear then charged sticking and stabbing this monster keeping away from its deadly mouth and claws. The fear of them dying brought about courage and strength they never knew they had together. No one could get in a good fatal stab; this brute was still growling with Hank's spear sticking from its neck, which seemed to only make it mad, but what they were doing was stopping this bear from advancing and making it lose ground by backing it away, but the creature still clawed at their spears that were longer than the bear's reach. All of a sudden there was a sound like air under pressure escaping from something. Then a white, smoky mist of a cloud engulfed the head of this nine feet giant.

Everyone was surprised to see Hank spraying the fire extinguisher in the face of the beast.

"Get down!" Hank yelled to the pack. The chemical was getting into the bear's eyes; it couldn't see and continued walking backwards, but the whole time swinging its massive claws blindly. Hank proceeded spraying, forcing this deadly animal out the cave, than the contents within the extinguisher ran out. Hank swore silently to himself and threw the canister at the beast. It hit the bear in the head, but with no harmful effect. Hank didn't have time to wonder what to do next; what he did know was no one wanted this man killer to recover. The rest of the pack yelled a battle cry charging the giant with their spears causing it to take another step back. It lost its footing falling from the cave's small cliff landing on its head breaking the beast's neck; death was instant. Everyone was sad about the death of Wilson; his body was placed back on the travois inside the cave and crying was heard through the night. Dawn came accompanied by dark clouds overhead giving signs that rain was still due to fall. Michael and Amanda were hugged up alongside Hank and Mae who were hugged up also. Van and Beth seemed to be developing more than a friendly relationship. Although, they weren't hugging they were relatively close to one another all night since they didn't have the firewood stocked up as usual. They decided to take shifts sleeping while two people stood watch. The last couple of hours Keith had stood guard alone now the others were stirring awake.

"We got to do something with the body before it begins to stink," said Keith.

"Do you have to call him a body? Can't you say Mr. Wilson's name?" Van spat. Michael saw Keith's face harden as he was standing over the group in the circle with his spear and Keith saw Michael shake his head for him to stay calm.

"Easy Van, we all are hurting, but different people deal with hurt differently. I'm sure Keith meant nothing by it," Michael said. It was decided since they had no tools to bury Mr. Wilson they would pile some wood and place Wilson and his travois on top and burn it. The burial by fire was done at daybreak down from the cave not far from where the bear had fallen. A few words of prayer were said as the fire consumed Wilson's body. Once this was over with, the pack vowed to remember this animal that had terrorized their sanctuary hours ago. They were in need to restock the food supply. A couple of days ago the group had given spear fishing a try when they made their water run, but no luck. No one seemed patient enough to stand still long enough. The few times they tried they were unsuccessful. They knew that when fish were under water it would be hard to spear one because water bends light creating an illusion, plus these fish were just too fast so they settled for the frogs they caught, took them to the cave, and cooked and ate frog legs. The scout's brought it to their attention that bear meat could be eaten.

"How ironic, the animal that was going to eat us soon will be eaten by us," Mae commented.

"Yeah, but how can we preserve it? That's a big bear which means a lot of meat. I'm sure the carcass will begin to rot and stink soon," Keith said.

"Your correct, we don't have chemicals to preserve the meat however, we can make it so the meat will keep by using smoke," informed Michael.

"Smoke it?" Amanda asked. All stood over this brute who had killed Wilson without regard for his life.

"Yeah, smoke is another way to cure meat or fish. Hank and I still have our knives so we can dress this bear out. Cut it into strips about one inch wide, ten inches long, and maybe an eighth of an inch thick; hang them on a stick and slow cook them over a fire for about eight hours. Exposing the meat to smoke should preserve it allowing us to eat off of it for maybe a week or so. We will need food for this trip anyway," explained Michael with excitement in his voice.

"What about the idea of scouting to check out that light source?" Beth asked.

"After everything that went on last night, me and Michael thought it best to secure the food first. In survival you should take advantage of advantages. Always secure what food you can; you never know where your next ration of food will come from. I realize we had planned to make our move today, but the one constant thing about out here in nature is things don't always go as planned. Let's take a full day to prepare and preserve the food and then get ready for this trip. Can we all agree to that?" Hank asked and everyone agreed.

"You two wasn't the only one making plans. Me and my girl Amanda thought we all should put it to a vote on the rest of us tagging along with you guys." Hank and

Michael exhibited no surprise; they knew sooner or later the rest of the pack would want to venture out.

"Okay by show of hands who wants to go?" Keith asked and it was unanimous.

"Okay then it's settled we all go, but first we learn the five P's," said Hank waiting to get a response.

"Alright I'll bite, what the five P's?" Mae asked. Michael and hank said the words at the same time, "proper-preparation-prevents-poor-performance," so let's get the things done today so tomorrow we'll be better prepared. You all get a good amount of wood up to the cave and Michael and I will start dressing the bear out. Get several long sticks so we can extend the meat over the fire, and as you guys go back and forth for wood. We'll be sending up pieces of meat so for now place the strips on the big rock inside the cave. You all see that tree over there? Hank asked as he pointed.

"What tree? There are so many," Van asked.

"The young ones their not mature yet, it's the one that is about ten feet tall. Many of them are clustered together looking like someone with an afro," Hank explained. It was as if a light bulb came on in their heads; they saw it now.

"We need a lot of that wood because it smokes good. It's called Tag Alder; you'll see it will also give the meat good flavor," informed Michael.

"I've never had smoked meat that didn't taste good," said Keith imaging what bear would taste like. By nightfall everyone was over worn. The many trips back and forth for wood, the cutting up the bear, preparing the meat to cook and store had made everyone exhausted. The wood pile was stocked up higher than it ever had been. The fire was blazing high with the pack sitting to the back of the cave feeling safe now enjoying the fruits of their labor kicking back chewing on bear meat. Hands and mouths were greasy from the bear's fat. Some of the cooked fat was saved in a few bottles to make homemade lanterns with shoestrings cut short for wicks.

"This meat…is either…very good or I'm…very hungry," Keith said between bites.

"Yeah…I think it's…the nastiest…thing I've ever tasted," Hank said while biting hinto the meat barbaric. His jaws were full and poking out with grease running down his chin while winking his eye at Mae. The group laughed; everyone had their fill and went to sleep. There was a light rain that morning after breakfast; the plan was to pack provisions for the trip. The bear jerky was dry so it would keep without going bad. It was decided not to come back to the cave, but to keep moving now that the group had food and water to last for some time. Most of the day they traveled in the direction the light source was spotted. The land they traveled was thick with brush and trees and all sorts of different vegetation. They were getting ready to stop for a break when Van veered from the line they were walking and craned his head to the side. About fifty yards to their left looked like some sort of structure or a doorway of some kind. It was manmade, boarded up with some wood plants nailed together, and vegetation had grown around it was like a fifteen foot hill came up from the ground with a doorway.

"What is it Van?" Hank asked.

"It appears to be an entrance to an abandoned coal mine. Tourism is a major industry in this state, but the real cash comes from Wyoming mining which means there are many coal mines in this state. When the mines stop putting out so to speak the company moves on," Van answered.

"Good, something made by man means we could be close to civilization right?" Keith asked.

"Not necessarily; companies don't dig mines for the comfort of being close to home, they dig mines where the resources are," Van said.

"But even with that doesn't that mean that people still will be coming this way that could help us?" Beth asked. Van didn't want to spoil her hopes of being rescued, but at the same time he didn't want to lie to her either. He said, "take a look at the growth of these weeds at the opening; I doubt anyone has been out here for years so no we are still on our own."

"We've covered some miles, what do you all think about making this our base camp for tonight?" Michael asked. Everyone agreed and began to pull the boards from the opening. Once that was done they could see part of the way inside it slanted downwards; beyond that was total darkness.

"Van fill us in on coal mines, give us the do's and don'ts," Hank asked. Suddenly, Amanda screamed feeling like red hot needles were in her flesh. She went down to the ground holding her ankle.

"Amanda, what's wrong?" Michael asked with concern in his voice as he came to her aide. Two punctured wounds were just above ankle accompanied by two blood drops. The fear on her face showed the seriousness of what she was pointing at. It was something on the ground. They seen it; the snake that had bitten her was scurrying away through the brush.

Chapter 10

Amanda blinked back tears looking at the two small holes above her ankle.

"I have a cavity so I can't suck the poison out," said Michael never taking his eyes from the path of the snake.

"Go, I've seen what they do on westerns when someone gets snake bit. I'll do what must be done," answered Keith. Michael didn't have time to question him; her life could be hanging in the balance. Michael moved out to catch this varmint. Hank handed Keith his knife saying," everyone stayed with her; kept her lying down. Amanda tried not to move because the poison will spread quicker." Suddenly he started out behind Michael. Michael had already gone through the bush in search of the snake that may have ended Amanda's life. The first aid kit didn't contain any anti-venom serum and they were miles from anywhere, but he felt he must do what he can to help. Keith sat down on the ground taking Amanda's leg.

"This is gonna hurt," he said using Hank's knife to cut from one puncture wound to the other. Amanda clenched her teeth as he lanced her skin. She fought back the scream with Mae holding her still. Keith was being careful not to make the incision too deep. Mae was right there holding her hand for support. Keith began to suck on the wound, spitting it out quickly every time and being careful not to swallow the potential poison.

*

Michael seen the serpent making its way, but it was moving fast through the underbrush. All that could be seen was the tail of this serpent disappearing under and around vegetation with Michael in hot pursuit. His spear was in hand at the ready and Hank was right on Michael's heels. Branches were slapping each of them in their faces, but they kept their eyes on the ground chasing this reptile. Hank tripped falling down only to get back up continuing the chase not far behind Michael. Every time Michael was within striking distance, this creature evaded him. It was of paramount importance to catch this snake to recognize its markings so it could be determined if it was poisonous. Michael was beginning to tire; his lungs felt as if they were burning. Hank caught up to him and was equally as tired. Finally, they came across a big, fallen log blocking their path. The serpent was trapped; Michael and Hank raised their spears overhead to swat this unsightly creature on the ground. The snake's swiftness surprised them both when it quickly sprang from its coiled position striking Michael in his leg bringing him down to the ground. Hank missed hitting it by inches. His spear came in contact with the ground bringing up dirt close by the serpent. This big, spiral form was darting its forked tongue in and out to taste the air. When it opened its mouth, Hank saw the fangs of this reptile who knew how to use its tapering body. The snake was fast; it struck Hank in his arm before he could bring his hand back.

Everyone was still at the entrance of the mine; all were close to Amanda. Mae was sitting on the ground with Amanda's head in her lap consoling her. Keith had done all he felt he could do and was standing by the others still spitting and constantly rinsing his mouth with water from the water bottle he held in hand. All eyes were on Amanda. Suddenly, Hank and Michael stumbled into view and fell to the ground in front of the group taking in big gulps of air and making sounds as if they were in pain. Michael held up a lifeless form dangling from his hand. It was the dead snake with a smashed head. The blood from the snake was running down Michael's hand. They also noticed something else about the two scouts; both of them had what appeared to be multiple bumps in their face and hands along with some dark worms on them, wet, and muddy. Hank and Michael were in such discomfort they were sucking air through clenched teeth. At that point, Mae and

Amanda went to their scouts' side. When the young men finally caught their breath, Michael stood then helped Hank to stand. Michael held the snake up high overhead shaking it in victory. Amanda jumped up at the sight of this snake being so close to it.

"False alarm everyone this snake isn't poisonous," said Michael pointing to the underside of the snake's tail holding it for all to see.

"Look at the rings that go around the tail; they break when they meet. This means it's not poisonous. Now on the other hand, if the rings make a complete circle without breaking it's a poisonous snake.

"Thank God!" Amanda cried. Michael held the snake up in the sunlight with tow hands over his head in triumph.

"You see, together we can survive, and we will make it out of here together. As for this snake, we can clean this thing and eat…" Before Michael could finish his sentence everyone heard a loud, high piercing screech overhead that made them duck low from a reflexive flinch response as the thief snatched the serpent from Michael's hand.

"Damn!" Was their response. There was a stunned silence; it was a large eagle holding the snake in its talons making its get-a-way soaring high. The wing span was wider than any of them tall; the flapping of the wings made noise. Everyone was befuddled how smooth this great bird had been. Michael shook his head in amazement. It must have been stalking prey from miles above and seen an easy meal. When the eagle disappeared from their view they had a good laugh. Although, it hurt for Michael and Hank to laugh, they couldn't help themselves. The guys were saying how cool it was and how they wished the eagle taking the snake could have been caught on camera, but since the phones didn't work the camera on them was out of the question. The talk among the girls was hopefully this big bird didn't come back and try to carry one of them away. Their pack had decided to camp the entrance of the mine. They soon learned about the bumps and discomforting pain the scouts were feeling. Michael and Hank explained how they both had been got snake bitten and Michael had struck the fatal blow that killed the snake. In their rush to get back and tell the good news about the snake not being deadly, they stopped to rest and catch their breath leaning on this tree for support not realizing they had disturbed a wasp's nest. The wasps felt threatened and violently defended themselves. Out of this big nest they came in hundreds viciously stinging the young men as they ran for their lives. Michael still held the dead snake when they dived into a nearby river.

"Yeah, I know the feeling I've been stung by bees before, but they never left marks on me like the ones I see on you guys," said Keith.

"Well, there is a big difference; when a bee stings its stinger is barbed and often it stays in whatever it stings, but the bee will die afterwards. Now the wasp is a nasty little bugger; its stinger is straight like a sword allowing it to stab you over and over again without it dying." All were in a circle with the scouts in the process of getting a fire started when Hank looked closer at Michael saying," man, you've got leeches on your neck." Upon closer inspection from Amanda; she saw the repulsive looking things which in turn made Mae take a look at Hank and there they were. The mud had hid their presence. Both girls' expressions told it all; Hank knew he had leeches too. Everyone was inspecting the two as if they were germs under a microscope.

"Can't we pull them off you guys?" Keith asked.

"We could, but there is a chance of ripping leeches head off in our skin, and that's the part with the teeth. We'll get this fire started and get a couple of you to burn them off with the hot end of a twig," explained Michael. It was plain to see that Hank was uneasy.

"You okay buddy?" Michael asked.

"I hate leeches; I'll be okay once we get these blood suckers off me. Just knowing they are on me robbing me of my blood makes my skin crawl." Hank cringed at the thought of it.

"How can you guys not know these things have bit into your skin and sucking on you? I can't understand that?" Beth asked. Hank was getting ready to say something when he was interrupted "may I?" Hank nodded his head.

"As with most creatures that steal blood they have a chemical that deadens the skin so you won't feel the bite. This allows them to dine at their leisure," answered Michael.

"Okay, that makes sense, but that still doesn't make them any less hideous," said Beth showing her unpleasantness towards them. Once inside the scouts moved quickly to build the fire from hitting the back of their knives on a hand held rock making sparks ignite tender. It smelled of coal oil, rust, and was mixed with a musty odor. What could be seen consisted of dirt and timber with cross beams overhead for support. The fire was made; the leeches were removed and thrown into the fire. Now the group set around the fire eating bear jerky. Since they had removed the boards to enter the mine it was an open view to the outside. The clouds had opened up and the rain came down hard and heavy. Lightning flashed briefly lighting up the inside of the mine. Amanda looked at Keith and said," Keith, thank you very much for your help. Even if the snake wasn't poisonous you put in the effort to save my life. I appreciate you."

"Today, I can say that you are welcome Amanda, I'm used to doing for myself, but being with you all in life and death situations have changed all of that. Besides, I didn't have any cavities for the poison to seep into and I was the closest to you. I made the right choice. I've said it before I like this pack thing. It's as if we are...family," Keith reveals. Everyone had seen the change in Keith. Michael tapped his best friend on the shoulder making sure everyone hears him say, "you see Hank we get snake bit and stung stabbed by hundreds of angry wasp and what do we get?" While winking his eye at Keith.

"Give me a chance I was gonna my way around to you too," Amanda said then she thanked and hugged Hank.

"Girl, get your paws off my man. All of his hugging is for Hank's gal, me," Mae said jokingly. Hank was embarrassed this caused laughter.

"Come here Michael, I saved the best for last." Then Amanda flew into his arms with a strong hug and her lips finding his. The group hooted and hollered with joy. After some more bear jerky Hank and Michael thought it best to go out in the rain to wash the mud off. Before they knew it the whole pack was out in the rain with them playing in it. Shortly after that they were back around the fire.

"That wasn't a bad idea everyone getting some water on them. It was starting to smell ripe up in here," said Mae to the other girl's.

"Yeah, a good, hot bath is still at the top of my list when we get out of here," Amanda added.

"Girl, I know that's right, I want so many bubbles in the tub they overflow onto the floor," Mae imagined.

"You girls can keep the bubbles. I want scented oils in my bath where I can immerse myself completely and just lose myself," added Beth.

"You had me sold with the oils until you said lose yourself," said Mae.

"Why do you say that?" Beth asked.

"I can answer that; because we are already lost," answered Amanda. Keith decided to change the subject.

"Where do you guys think this mine leads? Van you seem to know more about these things what's your thoughts?" Keith asked.

"We can't be sure. What I can tell you is we ran the risk of a cave in or a drop-off also some of the gas could prove to be fatal. Either it could injure or kill us," answered Van.

"You really are a bookworm huh?"

"The risk is too high to even attempt such a feat," reasoned Hank. All had agreed to get through the night and resume their search for the unknown light. Hopefully, tomorrow weather permitting. The following morning the group packed up and were on their way; unknown to them eyes were watching them from the bush; human eyes.

Chapter 11

The rain stopped and sun began to peek through the clouds. The day had begun to heat up; animalistic sounds from different species were heard from time to time during their travel. The pack stayed alert knowing danger could come from any concealed place out here at any given time. Soon they came to the edge of the woodlands; here the group took a break looking out from the trees across miles of desert that had welcomed the rain. No one thought crossing this wasteland would be a good idea. Van pointed to a very tall, gray rock formation off in far distance miles away.

"It's called the Devil's Tower; the elevation is over a thousand feet above the Belle Fourche River, which means we should be in Eastern Wyoming. It's also a sacred site for Native Americans," Van informed.

"How are we looking on water?" Hank asked the girls.

"Four bottles left after everyone finishes the bottle they have," answered Beth.

Keith smelled it first, then the others smelled it too; the smell of smoke in the air. Someone definitely had a campfire going nearby. The thought of being rescued fueled their movements to travel through the dense growth of plants much faster until they came upon an area where they could see through the vegetation. Finally, the pack seen people; this brought a feeling of gladness and relief. There were three men in this camp. What they seen next made them get down and remain silent. The two men were facing the one, the elder of the three held a gun on the one. The pack's sense of rescue and relief was replaced with fear when the elder man shot the other man in cold blood, then put the gun back into its holster on his hip. The group was startled at the loud sound of gunfire. Beth turned her head away from what she had just witnessed and began to cry out loud. Van was there to put his hand over her mouth.

Everyone hoped the man with the gun hadn't heard anything, but they knew that you can't un-ring a bell. The man with the gun lifted his brow looking in their direction.

"Paw, did you hear that?" One of the men asked.

"Yeah I heard who's out there?" Buck if that's you I've never known you to be so noisy with all that training you had," said the older man with a southern drawl. Hank whispers to the group, "who is this Buck he's talking about?" Suddenly from behind they hear the unmistakable click of a gun being cocked.

"I'm Buck!" Surprised everyone turned to see a man dressed in camouflage, holding a rifle on them. He was concealed well with the natural surroundings. No one had noticed him; this guy was good. The pack was marched into camp at gunpoint, patted down for weapons, and then made to sit in a row with their hands on top of their heads facing their captures. Their knives, spears, and phones were taken from them. Buck liked the stone made knives so he kept them and the father held onto Hank and Michael's knives. The spears and their useless phones were thrown into the fire. The elder of the men walked around them looking them over and then said," you all are a bunch of kids. What in tar-nation are you doing way the hell out here anyway?" Michael thought it best to be honest, he just seen this man take a life.

"Can we put our arms down?" The man nodded yes. One of the younger woodsmen started to walk away from camp with the rest of them looking confused. The elder gave him a look of disapproval, you could hear it in his voice when he asked, "Jed where the heck you think your going boy?"

"Paw, I figured since we got woman folk thought I'd go to our truck and grab some beer and condoms so we all could have a good time, that is if you know what I mean," said Jed winking his eye with a devilish grin and blood shot eyes. The elder was chewing on some tobacco,

154

he seen this made the kids tense up, one even balled up his fist. He spit a long stream of brown liquid on the ground.

"Jed come here boy." Jed comes to see what his father wanted.

"Yeah paw." His father had shot out fast slapping Jed across the back of his head causing him to stumble.

"Are you plum stupid? We may do some illegal things, but we're not monsters. Get your half witted hide back over there with your brother. The rest of y'all pay him no mind. Now who are you and what you doing out here?"

"We were in a horrible bus crash some days ago, we've been doing all we can just to stay alive. We just want to go home me and Hank here had some outdoor training and we're boy scouts. The rest of our group here is a man…" The man in the camo interrupted Michael pointing to each one of them. "Amanda, Beth, Mae, Keith, Van, and you just gave us you twos names." This bewildered the group; they wondered how could he have known their names?

"Well since we know your names it's only fair that you know ours. I'm the father of those boys you see here. My name is Merle, you've met Buck he's my oldest boy. He's been in the military; a sniper of some kind special forces. He doesn't speak much though; this is the most I've heard him speak in a long time."

"But how did he know our names?" Keith asked.

"Mind your tongue young man; it's impolite to interrupt when I'm speaking. I've killed men for less. You can ask Buck that question yourself when I'm done. Where was I…? Oh yeah this here is Jed, he means well, but he lives to smoke them weeds, brains seem to fried at times, no ambition. That stuff makes him as dumb as a fence post. He's my youngest boy sometimes it's as if his engine is running, but clearly no one is behind the wheel, you know what I mean? His light is on, but no one's home." Hank pointed to the dead man on the ground several yards away.

"What was his name?" The pack was shocked all these men had rifles strapped to their backs. For a brief moment silence hung in the air, only the crickets could be heard. Merle gave Hank a hard look; it was as if time stood still. Then as sudden as it came, his whole demeanor changed, a smile tugged at Merle's lips and he began laughing and his son's joined in laughing with him, nothing at this point was funny to the pack, they just wanted to get away from these madmen. After a good laugh, the band of back woodsman got back serious, but Jed the weed head was still laughing uncontrollably smacking his knee and making a spectacle of himself with all eyes on him until Merle went over to him and slapped him across his face.

"Dag nabit, what did you go and do that for Paw?" Jed asked rubbing his stinging face. Merle ignored him and looked at Hank.

"I've got to give it to you dark-skinned young man; you've got a set of them on you. Smart, I like, sassing your elder I don't. That there was Clem, we had an argument, and let's just say I strongly disagreed with him, needless to say I won the argument," Keith raised his hand to be called on.

"Yeah go ahead boy, have your say," said Merle.

"Buck, how did you know our names?" Buck looked at his father for approval to answer, Merle nodded his head yes.

"I've been following y'all since you left our mine. I was close enough at times to reach out and touch you so being within earshot I heard y'all call others by their names. Paw, they were inside the mine," said Buck. We had no idea we were trespassing in your mine it looked abandon. We only went inside for shelter," Michael explained.

"You see young fella, your transgressions goes much farther than just trespassing. You have seen me kill Clem over there. Now that makes you all a witness. I can't and won't allow anyone to go to the law," said Merle with fire in his voice.

"Witness! I'm no witness, I'm a Christian," said Hank using humor to cope with the situation. Jed busted out with laughter, saying between laughter, "I get it, Jehovah Witness!" Then continued laughing. Merle went over and back-handed Jed off his feet; then went over and stood in front of Hank.

"Still a comedian huh?" Suddenly he punched him in the stomach. Hank folded over from the blow as air left his lungs. The rest of the group motioned to charge Merle. They all stopped short when he pulled his gun and cocked the hammer back. Even Buck took careful aim and would shoot if his paw gave the word. Merle holstered his gun.

"You youngins are coming with us. Where are the rest of the folks that was with you?" "Dead! They are all dead, just like that man you killed over there. Who are you people anyway?"

Beth shouted loudly with tears running down her face. She seen Merle smile at her then suddenly his features went stone cold as he pulled his side arm and took aim at her.

Chapter 12

The long barreled gun barked loud causing Beth to jump, cringe, and close her eyes tight. At the same time, the .44 bullet went slightly left of Beth hitting its target twenty-five yards behind her. The moose bellowed and went down hard causing a small cloud of dust to whirl up from the impact. The pack was in panic mode thinking Beth had been shot until they heard then seen the downed animal behind her. It was a welcomed relief knowing Beth was okay. All of them looked at this mad man with smoke still coming from his gun. Beth opened her eyes when he walked past her to make sure the moose was dead holding his big gun in the air saying, "never forget that this barks louder than any of you." Merle walked over to the moose, nudged it with his foot making sure it would never move on its own again.

"Buck you keep the kids covered. Jed come over here and help me to dress out this meat so the youngins can help us carry it back to our camp." Jed had brown hair down to his shoulders. He wore a turtle neck sweater along with some casual cargo pants. On this face were round wire frame glasses; he had the look of a hippy from back in the sixties. They packed up all that could be carried and were on their way with merle and his son's keeping their guns on the group as they hiked through the trees in silence.

"Didn't Jed mention something about you guys having a truck?" Michael asked breaking the silence.

"That's good you pay attention when people talk. Take a page from their book boys, yeah we have a truck, but old Betsy done ran her course. I know for a fact the engine is done for. I examined her myself so we'll stop and get what we can out of her and head to our camp," said Merle as they walked. They came to some beat up, rust eaten truck that had seen better days. Jed and Buck salvaged what they could from the truck then everyone was ushered through the woods. Merle was a tall, thin man of sixty-five years old with a gray beard that was a bit scraggly. His skin was weathered and had the look to be as tough as his red, unkempt hair that was medium length. The disgusted look on these youngins' faces told Merle that they didn't want to be carrying dead moose remains. Beth slipped and Van put his burden down and helped her to her feet.

"You okay Beth?"

"Yeah, I just feel so tired and look at this moose blood dripping everywhere," said Beth with disgust as she went to pick up her load. Van stopped her and picked it up for her and attempted to carry hers and his.

"Well, I'll be! Ain't that cute; we got a love struck pup in this litter. Boy that darn love bug done went and bit you huh boy?" Jed asked with a twig hanging from his mouth. Van tried to carry her load and his, but it was too much for him. His knees buckled, Van went down on one knee still holding the meat on both shoulders, and Jed couldn't help, but to laugh. Merle watched as the pack went over to help Van carry the extra weight he had gotten from Beth. When the pack had divided it among themselves, they continued being marched along with the woodsmen. Merle marveled at how keen these youngins were from the short time he'd been around them. On the other hand, they would need to be watched closely. He spoke loud enough for everyone to hear, "that was pretty impressive how you all helped each other back there. I can see how you survived out here. Son's that's another page you take from their book; you'll always be stronger together than apart. You kids should know that moose I shot could have hurt or killed any one of us you know. They've been known to charge a moving train, knows no fear; mean cuss those animals."

"How much farther Mr. Merle?" Michael asked.

"Right over that yonder," said Merle pointing to the hill. About a quarter mile beyond the hill they came to a camp with a large military tent that you could walk around inside and a smaller one beside it. A nice-sized campfire was going; some clothes were hanging on the nearby trees close to the tents. From the look of things, these woodsmen had been camping here for some time.

"All of you drop your load over here." After doing so their hands and feet were tied and then made to sit on this log that wasn't far from the fire.

"Buck, I want you to go get rid of Clem's body then check our back trail and several miles out from the way they came. Make sure they aren't being followed or looked for," ordered Merle.

"Their footprints should be easy to pick up. What do you want me to do if I run across anyone looking for them?" Buck asked.

"Make sure they don't follow anyone else. Remember three people can keep a secret if two of them are dead." With that Buck melted back into the woods where he felt the most at home. Then Merle turned to Jed, pointing his finger at him.

"You are to remain here and keep an eye on these youngins. Nothing and I do mean nothing bet not happen to them."

"Paw do I have to rat now? We've been going strong all day long. I need some sleep paw."

"Boy you gone do it rat now, don't have me to tell you again. You'll get enough sleep when your dead. Let's tie them up first; then I'm gonna make us something to eat, and process the meat." Jed took a seat on a nearby stump facing the youngins while his dad began preparing the moose meat.

"What are we gonna do?" Van whispered.

"I don't know, but these sure are some country talking, deranged backwoods men got the drop on us youngins as Merle would say," said Michael.

"What do you all think they are doing out here like this?" Amanda asked.

"I'm not sure, but more importantly what they gonna do with us?" Mae asked.

"Did anyone notice that there is a woman or women somewhere about?" Hank asked.

"How would we know such a thing?" Mae asked.

"Because some of the clothes on those trees are not a man's," Hank replied. Everyone looked and seen clothes hanging on the trees, but the one thing that stood out now were a couple of bras.

"Okay so what, I see a female's under clothes," said Keith.

"So there is a good chance that there are more of them," said Michael. Suddenly, movement was heard coming through the woods; their eyes searched to see what was coming their way. Jed had nodded out with his rifle in hand and Merle was busy with the meat. No one said it, but each of the youngins thoughts' gave way to the possibility that it could be a wolf, or bear. Something that could rip them to shreds and here they were tied up. A sigh of relief escaped their lips when a young woman appeared and walked into the camp. Her face was dirty along with the blue jeans and shirt she wore. This female had a compound bow strapped to her back and a Tarzan knife tied to her thigh, and in her hands she carried five dead squirrels. She seen seven strangers tied up sitting on the log and stared at them for a brief moment.

"Paw!" She yelled causing Jed to jump awake pointing his rifle in all different directions.

"Over here Tabby," answered Merle.

"Jed put that gun down for you go and hurt somebody boy," said the young woman walking away from Jed over to her father.

"Who are they and why you got them all trussed up," she asked.

"Just some young interlopers in the wrong place at the wrong time. You're just in time to help me preserve and cook something for supper," answered Merle. She placed the squirrels down close to the moose meat then said, "I guess these little vermin's' can wait. Let me take a closer look at our guests." She walked over to the group sitting on the log and standing over them looking at each one. This also allowed the group to get a closer look at her. Although, her face was smudged with dirt, it was evident this young woman was good looking. Keith was smitten with love at first sight. It was as if she had taken all the air from outside because he found it hard to breathe, and she was breath-takingly beautiful. The group was thinking to themselves how this woman that none of them had seen before had the power to knock big Keith over with a feather. She stood there by Keith and noticed him taking in breathes deeply and turning cherry red in the face.

"Paw, do they really need to be tied up? This one looks sick or something." She removed her big, long blade from the sheath then cut Keith's ropes. He stood rubbing his wrists attempting to regain the circulation in his arms. He was able to calm his breathing and managed to say," thank… thank you!" She gave him a smile and put her knife away; their eyes met.

"Your nice and easy on the eyes their big fella. My name is Tabitha what's yours?"

"Keith," he said looking down at his feet.

"I see you're a bashful one aren't you?" Before he could answer Merle was coming their way.

"Daughter of mine or not you don't run nothing here, I call the shots," said Merle walking towards them with the bloody knife in his hands he had been using to cut up the moose meat. Once Keith was able to tear his stare from hers he seen Merle with the bloody knife. The look on

Merle's face caused Keith to back away towards the dense growth of trees.

"Boy, you try to escape I'll cut you four ways long, deep, wide, and repeatedly." Keith didn't need to hear no more, before he knew it his feet were propelling him forward at a fast pace. Keith ran into the woods with the group cheering him on. Jed took careful aim with his rifle to shoot Keith. Tabitha was there; she forced Jed's rifle upwards when he pulled the trigger his shot went wild in the air. Then she turned her attention to her father as he now stood with her and Jed.

"Paw, see what you done went and did. He was more scared of you than a fish is of a skillet," said Tabitha getting upset.

"Tabby didn't have to take his ropes off and don't you ever ruin my shot again you little stupid heifer," shouted Jed close to Tabitha's face then slapped her spinning her head around. Merle stood by and watched; he believed in letting his children work things out among themselves. Tabitha turned facing Jed with a small drop of blood on her bottom lip. She gave him a gut shot doubling Jed over then her knee found his forehead lifting him from his feet landing flat on his back dropping the rifle. Merle picked up the rifle and faced Tabitha.

"Get your tomboy behind out there and find that youngin. Fix this Tabby, now get!" Merle shouted and Tabitha went through the vegetation after him.

Merle then turned to the group, "don't be foolish like your friend who took off. I'm not into nursing kids, I'd rather just shoot you, and get it over with, but I must be patient and see if anyone is out there looking for any of you. Jed get posted back up and watch them while I finish what I'm doing. That youngin better hope Tabby finds him before some of them wild critters get a hold of his hide.

*

Keith didn't know where he was running to; he just couldn't get the image out of his mind that a psycho was coming at him with a bloody knife. He had to keep going; then his new friend came to mind that he left behind. He felt his lungs beginning to burn. Who was that pretty female that seemed to possess a certain power over him? Thoughts of her distracted him from not watching his footing when he tripped downward rolling through dead leaves, pine needles, dirt, and tall grass until the land came to an end. Suddenly, airborne he felt himself falling out of control with arms and legs waving wildly with gravity pulling him down fast to belly flop into a raging river. The coldness caused Keith to suck in a deep breath and the current dragged him along. The young man did all he could to remain afloat and keeping his head above water. He went along bobbing up and down but manage to see a tree with a low hanging branch.

"If I could just grab a hold of that when this river carries me under it, I'll have one chance to grab it," he says to himself. The powerful current slung him around like a rag doll. Land was close on both side, but it may as well have been miles away for every effort he tried was in vain. The low hanging branch was coming, "I… must…time this right." Keith reached up with all he had grabbing the low, hanging branch raising himself up enough to breathe properly, but didn't have enough strength to pull himself from the water. He hung there with half of his body still in the water for what seemed a lifetime. The raging river was loud; sounded like a thousand voices were yelling at him. The water also seemed to be angry. He closed his eyes and held on for life. Was someone yelling at him? When he opened his eyes he didn't see anyone. The hands were beginning to hurt from holding up his weight coupled with the pull of the water. The flow of this river was relentless, but Keith refused to be pulled from the safety of this branch. There seemed to be movement on the same branch he was hanging on. The constant splash of the water in his eyes made it hard to see. As it got closer he recognized it to be a huge spider. Keith had no idea if it was poisonous or not. What was visibly frightening was its talon like fangs. The last thing he needed now was to be spider bitten with those hypodermic needles for fangs. The young man yelled at this spider as it neared closer, but his yelling had no effect on the arachnid. The realization came to him that this thing lived right above this loud river so it had to be use to noise. Keith made a decision before the giant spider got to his hand. He released his hand on the limb. This limb no longer supporting weight; bends back to its original position flinging the spider skyward. The fast moving current gave no mercy as it pulled Keith into the white water rapids. Being forced against a big boulder and bumping his head he was no longer able to stay afloat. He felt himself sinking as he was carried along with water

rushing inside his nose and mouth before he lost all
consciousness.

Chapter 13

Jed had went back to sleep in a sitting position with rifle in hand pointing at the teenagers. The group talked in a low whisper, "you guys think Keith is going to be alright?" Van asked.

"I don't know, but it seems as if we are running into things right after the other, constantly being challenged," added Mae.

"I hope Keith and the rest of us make it out of this mess, I'm thankful we are still living," said Amanda.

"But what if we don't make it? What if we all die out here? Who would know?" Beth asked hanging her head.

"We are not going to die out here, so remove those self defeating thoughts from your head," Michael said with conviction. He had been sitting apart from the rest on the ground using a jagged rock to cut the rope that tied his hands. Hank was keeping an eye on Merle to let Michael know when he was coming. Michael was cutting his rope, but keeping his eyes on the man sleeping in front of them with the rifle. Beth seen what was going on and said, "maybe that's not such a good idea." Michael felt the rope give then he sat back on the log with the rest of them keeping his hands behind his back.

"Beth we must do what we can to get away from these people, "Michael explained.

"I'm scared and I just want to go home," Beth managed to say with tears in her eyes.

"We are all scared and want to go home to be with our loved ones, but in order to go home to be with our loved ones we might have to do some things we don't like or have never done before. Keep in mind Merle is a killer, we witnessed him kill a man in cold blood. Do you want to be here when his son Buck gets back and reports no one is following us then he can kill us with no law to investigate?

Do you want to be around for that?" Michael asked and Beth hung her head again saying, "no".

"What must we do?" Amanda asked.

"Yeah I'm down with whatever must be done to get us out of here in one piece," added Mae.

"Count me in," Van chimed in.

"So what's the plan?" Hank asked.

"Now that I'm no longer tied I say lay hands on Jed here and take the gun he has and shoot him and Merle."

Michael's intention was to go over to Jed and do what he had to do. Hank knew this and hooked his leg around Michael's ankle to prevent him from standing. He looked at Hank with disappointment.

"Michael we can't kill anyone in cold blood, that's not what we stand for."

"And I can't allow them to come after us once we escape either," reasoned Michael.

"I'm with you friend of mine, I will do what must be done to stop them from harming any of us, but there has to be another way," whispered Hank.

"I know your right; these conditions we're under makes me desperate I guess, I wouldn't be any better than them if I do what they do, I'll untie you all and we'll take it from there," said Michael as he stood keeping his eyes glued on the man across from holding the gun. Jed's eyes blinked a few times slowly before he became awake. Jed saw Michael standing there and managed to say, "what the!" Michael didn't give him time to gain his senses. He dived hitting Jed in his chest with his shoulder. Both men went to the ground trying to gain control of the rifle. Both stood doing their best to take the gun from the other's grasp. Michael was quicker and had better balance. The rifle was twisted from Jed's hands hitting him across his jaw with the butt end of it causing Jed to go down hard yelling from the pain. Michael now stood with rifle in hand breathing hard.

"Michael run, they won't kill us knowing a witness to the murder is out there," said Hank. Michael hesitated not wanting to leave them. Merle seen what was going on and ran making his way towards them closing the distance.

"Run!" The pack yelled at Michael. Michael knew he had to return for them, he took off giving them his back at break neck speed, running with rifle in hand. Merle had made it to where the rest of them were tied. He stopped removed his gun taking careful aim at Michael's back. At the time of him pulling the trigger; Van's foot shot out kicking Merle behind his knee in the crook of his leg causing Merle to go off balance. The gun fired sending the bullet high over Michael's head, than he disappeared into the woods with the group cheering him on. Merle holstered his revolver, stepped to Van and back-handed him twice. A trickle of blood escaped Van's bottom lip. Jed looked up to see Merle extending his hand, helped him up to his feet only to be back-handed back to the ground.

*

Michael ran as fast as his legs would carry him, knowing his life depended on it. When he heard the shot he knew that bullet was meant for him. Adrenalin fueled his movements through the dense bushes, shrubs, and trees. He did his best to remember the way he ran so he could return and help the others. Michael found it difficult to run. The thickness of these plants was incredible. The scout had put some distance between him and the camp, but constantly looking around behind himself as he ran with gun in hand. All of a sudden to his surprise the ground changed to a steep downgrade; the slant was so downward he tumbled and cursed himself for not paying attention to his footing. He rolled down this hill losing the rifle and not being able to control his speed of descent. Michael prayed he wasn't rolling to his death.

Chapter 14

Keith slowly awakened to an intense throbbing pain in his head. His throat and nostrils were stinging from the water that was rushing out of him followed by a series of cough to clear his airways. Keith realized he was sitting alongside of the river bank with some female on her knees leaning him forward patting his back hard. Once he recovered the young man scrambled to his feet trying to regain his bearings.

"Hold on their big fella, I just saved your life," said Tabitha.

"Big fella, I won't chase you any farther especially after dragging your heavy hide from that there river. I'm tired and I'll shoot you in the leg with an arrow first. Besides, you may not make it too far with that goose egg of a knot you got on your head. Your likely to pass out and become food for some animals," she warned. Keith stopped in his tracks just hearing about becoming a meal for animals. He had a brief flashback to that enormous spider. Suddenly, he became dizzy putting his hand on his head trying to balance himself. She went to his side to ease him to the ground against a tree in a sitting position and sat there beside him.

"What's your name big fella?"

"Keith, thank you for pulling me from my death; that river seemed as if it was angry at me."

"That river is angry at everyone," she said with a little chuckle.

"I banged my head pretty bad, I guess I owe you," he said while looking into her eyes. She was very attractive in ways he couldn't put into words.

"Yeah, big fella you owe me a bunch. Pulling you from that water was no picnic, and then I had to put my lips on yours to put breath back into you. And to make matters worse when you came to, you threw up in my mouth. That was no fun let me tell ya."

"You gave me mouth to mouth resuscitation?"

"Is that what you city folk call it?"

"Yes, but why did you save me?"

"I just did what had to be done. I'm gonna rinse my mouth out in the river. You rest up a bit." When she had finished she came and stood over Keith.

"I must get you back with the others so when you feel you can walk we'll go."

"Tabitha, I'm not going back to that camp with you and those crazy kin folks of yours."

"Keith, can you see those tracks coming from that dense growth of trees close to that river's edge?"

"Yeah, so what?"

"Those belong to some predators we don't want to be in the company of when they come to get a swig of that water over there. So the sooner you can move the better off we will be." Keith at this point didn't want to protest against her logic, not in his current state of condition. He

186

still felt a little dizzy, but could probably will himself to move from this dangerous spot. Yet he couldn't allow her to take him back to that crazed man. For now she was needed if only to make it away from this river bank where animals came for a drink until he could do better on his own he must allow her to help him. Keith stood and went to take a step and wobbled a bit. She went to his side, put his arm around her neck and they walked away. Their progress was slow yet they had traveled a good ways to an area where some partridge hens were scavenging for food. Their little heads were bobbing up and down constantly on the alert for predators. She sat him down alongside a tree and sat there with him as they took a rest.

"Keith, you see those little hens all about in that grass over yonder?"

"Yeah, you gonna shoot one of those cute little birds for us to eat I am starving."

"No, big fella those hens will alert us if some predator is coming. I'm hungry too; I have some jerky strips in my pockets. It's not enough to fill us up, but it's enough to make a turd." Keith gave a smile as she handed him some jerky. He liked the way she talked, she spoke her mind.

"Tabitha, why are you people living out here like this?" He asked in between bites of jerky.

"We have a cabin several miles from the campsite. We are many, many miles from any civilized folk. We camp out here for weeks on end from time to time to hunt for food, among other things and stuff like that, but of late paw has been more interested in the mine."

"Do you mean like a gold mine?" Keith asked.

"No silly, it's a coal mine has been tapped out for the longest. Heck that darn thing has been in their family for years."

"Their family? I thought Merle was your dad which would make that your family right?"

"I guess, but not in the real sense it's complicated."

"I don't understand since we are resting up a bit help me to understand."

"I will on one condition."

"What's the condition?" He asked.

"That you tell me all about how you and your people came to be tied up in our camp." Keith told her everything; the bus crash, the wolves, the thirst and hunger, and the biting bugs. Surviving the bear and how they had went on the move in search of rescue, came across a clearing with three men, how one of the men shot the other in cold blood, and the part about Buck surprising them and marching them all into camp.

"Tabitha, your father shot the other man and gunned him down. The guy didn't have a chance."

"You know the rest and how I came to be here with you." Tabitha's facial expression changed. She had the look of concern, fear, and then anger as she stood.

"What did the man look like that was shot?" She asked.

"This was my first time seeing anyone get shot, but he wasn't just shot, he was killed; it was too real. Do you honestly believe I would remember the details of what someone looked like," Keith said sharply.

"Okay, then what was he wearing?" Tabitha inquired.

"Really... now you want me to try and recall the clothes this man was wearing? Really!"

"Keith, I need to know what you know."

"Listen, I like you; you got the cute thing going on in a tomboyish kind of way. I don't mean to be insensitive, but I'm worried about my own life and the friends I left behind so forgive me if I can't remember any facial recognition or fashion statements at this time. All I know is a man got killed in front of me end of story, Clem was killed in cold blood," Keith said louder then he intended.

"Clem? Did say Clem?" She asked.

"Yeah, I don't forget names. Did you know him?" Keith asked.

Tabitha's strength drained from her legs, she dropped to her knees beside Keith throwing her compound bow from her back. She cupped her face in both her hands and cried hard. Keith didn't know this female, but had a strong urge to go put his arms around her and say that everything is gonna be alright; the lie most people say in a time like this. She continued to let the tears flow. It was apparent she was emotionally hurt bad. Obviously, it was from what he had told her; the sound of Tabitha's cry really pulled at his heart strings', but he knew there was nothing he could do or say to buffet the pain. He would let her ride it out uninterrupted and see which way it went. She went on crying for a while, then did some sniffles, and then tried to compose herself. Tabitha wiped her face on the sleeve of her jacket, stood, then picked up the compound bow, swung it to her back, then she looked at Keith with bloodshot eyes.

"We must go," she said.

"You gonna be okay?" He asked and she nodded her head yes.

He stood. "Look apparently you knew this Clem guy. That's none of my business, and I don't mean to be callused, but our deal was to tell me about you and your family after I told you about me and my friends," Keith reminded her. She began to survey their surroundings seriously with intense purpose. He seen she was currently distracted ignoring his question. She readied her bow with the deadly broad head arrow. She stared down the shaft for a target as the sun glistened off the razor blade head. Keith knew something was up, but didn't know what.

"What's wro...." He attempted to ask.

"Shhhh," was her only reply. Then all the hens took flight doing what could to be anywhere, but here. Something or some things were out there. Keith's thoughts were whatever was going on wasn't good. He slowly stood. Suddenly with blinding speed it came from concealment to the brush, low, hard, and fast at the two.

*

Michael's death defying tumble landed him at the bottom of the hill where the biggest portion of this land grew thorn bushes. His body protested from the stinging pain of the needles embedded in his body. Slowly, he sat up grimacing from the discomfort of the small spikes. He stood and began to remove the troublesome, annoying, prickly things. It proved to be pain staking and time-consuming, but finally he believed he had removed them all. Looking up to the hill from which he came. Clearly, it was far too many thorn plants to go back the way he came. Since that wasn't an option, what now? He had escaped the madman Merle, but what about his friends he thought. He could go on his own with hopes of finding some help and then come back for them, but how long would that take? Would his friends be hurt or worse yet killed in his absence? What could he possibly do to help them against men who had guns? All of these questions plagued him as he walked on feeling like a pin cushion and weaponless. They motivated him to make himself a rock knife and with it find a stick and make a sharp spear that would be his first order of business he thought to himself. Michael counted it as a blessing when he came across materials to make the rock knife and shortly afterward a spear. Within a couple hours he made the weapons that were needed. The rock knife was now tucked away in the waist band of his pants while he used the five foot long spear as a walking stick, and soon wandered across a river. He walked along the bank trying to collect his thoughts as to what action he must take to free his friends. He noticed several animal tracks; some small and others were big alerting him that this is not the place to be hanging out at too long. He walked faster knowing this and then seen more tracks, but these were human tracks. Footprints leading into the woodlands, Michael wasted no time following in the direction of the shoe impressions he seen left in the soft dirt.

*

Merle had moved the pack into the small stand up tent were no sharp stones or any other thing could cut ropes. This tent and the big one was a couple of the many things they had acquired from the military surplus store. Merle went from each one of them tightening and making sure their ropes were tied tight and they were sitting alongside the tent. Jed stood with his rifle in hand aimed at the group as he chewed on the twig that was hanging from his mouth. Once Merle was done checking their bonds he looked at them all then said, "ladies first." He reached down and snatched Beth to her feet only to slap her back to the ground. She cried; Merle repeated the slapping with all the females. When he was done with them he went over to Van, pulled him to his feet, then punched him in his stomach with much force doubling him over as he fell down moaning then up-a-chucked the contents of his stomach. When he lifted Hank to his feet, Hank decided to strike first. He head-butted Merle making Merle take a few steps back with his eyes watering. Merle felt his nose and seen blood on his hand; he had a nose bleed. Hank wished his hands wasn't tied; he was defenseless against Merle's assault. Merle repeated hitting Hank until he went to the ground, then he began kicking Hank in his stomach.

*

The hideous looking beast kept coming without pause with pointed teeth projecting outside its mouth. It was thirty yards away and closing the distance fast when Keith realized what this thing was charging at them. Fear washed over him knowing he couldn't outrun this creature. He hoped Tabitha was a good shot. At the same time he held his arms out in defense. It was making a grunting sound as if it was mad at them. Tabitha judged the distance and timed it just right before letting her arrow take flight. The arrow made a whispering sound until it found its mark in the head of the wild boar. The boar went down hard tumbling over itself, and then slid on its face to within eight feet of them never to move on its own again. Keith found it hard to believe his own eyes; in between breathing hard he said," good shot Tabitha."

"Yeah, but it's a shame we don't have time to cut and save this meat. These things make good eating," she said shaking her head while looking at this animal she had just taken the life of. She remembered Clem had taught her to only kill an animal when you had to eat or in self-defense. This was in self-defense, but knowing that still didn't bring her any comfort.

"I guess I should thank you for saving my life again."

"Yeah, your beginning to make this a habit," she said with a smile.

"I still want to hear your side of the story Tabitha."

"Okay, but let's walk and talk. There may be more of them, besides I need to sort this crap out," said Tabitha. She waited until she believed they were out of harm's way then explained to him about her mother being married to Merle.

"She died a couple years ago of some disease that I can't say right, but before she died she called me to her deathbed to have a woman to woman talk alone. She confessed sleeping with Merle's brother Clem who I thought was my uncle at the time. Merle married her soon after never knowing about my maw and his brother. She finally told me that Clem was my real dad. After one night in the hay of doing the wind thing together, nine months

198

later I was born into this world. They did some sort of test and turns out I'm Clem's daughter. Only my mother, Clem, and I know the real truth. It was kept a secret because it would have torn the family apart."

"I see why it saddens you about Clem. Do you believe Merle killed his brother because he found out about Clem and your mom?"

"No, silly my father was killed because of Merle's greed for money," said Tabitha.

"No disrespect Tabitha, but with the broke down truck and the rags I seen you all wearing, it's my guess your family don't see much money now or in your future."

"The family owns a mine that has been in their bloodline for generations."

"You mean like a gold mine?" Keith asked with lifted eyebrows.

"No silly it's a coal mine. At least once upon a time it was a coal mine. Since then it's been tapped out about a decade ago."

"How do you know all of this?" He asked.

"Because my real father told me. We talked when we could, but it would hurt me knowing we had to keep such a secret," she answered.

"Call me silly and stupid cause I don't get how a played out coal mine would be of any value Tabitha."

"You are absolutely correct a played out mine wouldn't have any value. Let me try to explain. When Merle and Clem's parents died, Merle was willed the mine and Clem the mineral rights. Not long ago oil was found under the mine."

"Okay Merle still is winning; he gets the best of both so why kill his brother?"

"Because whoever owns the mine owns what comes from the mine, but whoever owns the mineral rights owns all that's beneath the land," said Tabitha.

"About how much does Merle stand to gain now that he owns the mine and the mineral rights?"

"Nothing because Clem always told me and my maw he put me his only child in his will for everything he had that includes his mineral rights."

"Okay then Tabitha, I'll pose the same question to you. How much do you stand to gain with the oil below your land?" She was still processing the death of her father, and what she now must go through with Merle and his son's. The money factor never crossed her mind. She stopped and the realization struck her as she said in a soft voice.

"Millions!" Keith was bewildered with his mouth open.

Chapter 15

As, Michael went farther into the woods, he noticed it was teaming with life. Birds were feeding on bugs in the air and on the grass; squirrels were scurrying about on the tree limbs, even some small lizards were sun bathing on the rocks. The tracks Michael was following ended a ways back, falling down that hill had messed up his sense of direction as to which way to get back to the group. If he kept pressing forward he might find somebody or something to help. Questions went through his mind, asking himself, how could he go back to help his friends? Would they be hurt or worse? He wanted to see them all again, but holding Amanda in his arms was at the top of his list. He felt himself smiling. The smile went away quickly when he came across a badger in his path. Michael froze in his tracks not wanting this thing to feel threatened. He heard about the damage a badger could do with its claws and razor sharp teeth. The badger stood their perfectly still as they both looked each other over. It had long claws on the front feet, short legs, and grizzled fur. Badger's had reputations for being fearless and were gifted with speed. Michael decided to slowly back away. When he took a step back this seemed to enrage it because its lips curled up showing teeth, making a noise that sounded like air escaping from a tire. Michael gripped his spear with both hands, with the pointed end towards the badger. He calculated his chances; if this thing charged him he had one chance to spear it. If he missed, it could prove to be disastrous, with the speed this animal possessed, it would be all over him, relentless with its attack. To run was not an option, he must face this thing. A thought crossed his mind, he could throw the rock knife at the badger; the knife wouldn't stick in the badger, it would just need to distract it for a brief moment so he could stab it with his spear. Quickly, Michael removed the knife from his pants and threw it; it hit and bounced off the badger. To Michael's surprise before he could stab the badger with his spear, it shuffled off into the under bush. The scout did a silent prayer thanking God he didn't get hurt or have to hurt the badger. He went picked up his knife and returned it to his pants and continued to press forward.

*

Tabitha and Keith couldn't seem to agree on a plan of action. Keith wanted to free his friends and get far away from these people as people. Tabitha wanted revenge for her father against Merle, Buck, and Jed. She believed Keith when he told her that Merle sons didn't pull the trigger, but they were there when it happened, and didn't do anything to stop it from happening. She had seen the blind faith they had in Merle. She knew if Merle told any of his sons's to take a poop, they would squat and grunt. However, she on the other hand was known for going against him. Her untying Keith when she first seen him was proof of that. She was known in their family to be the tomboy rebel; she

204

just couldn't totally conform to his will. Now it was about revenge, she didn't care how they got what they had coming to them, just so they got it. Tabitha was waking fast, Keith could barely keep up with her; he still felt a bit dizzy. The money that she stood to gain from her father's death had been a fleeting thought; her anger for revenge overrode everything.

"Tabitha, come on, stop for a minute. Let's talk about this before we get to the camp," said Keith.

She stopped and faced him. "There is nothing to talk about big fella. The pointed end of my arrow goes through his heart, simple, and right as rain. I'm gonna do to them what they did to my paw. Some hillbilly justice is in order." Keith was looking her in her eyes then put both his hands on each of her shoulders.

"Listen, we can help each other if we stick together and help each other. My friends Michael and Hank help me to learn this. Please, we may only have one shot at this, we can both have what we want," he said with much sincerity. She searched his eyes for a long moment. Then her look softened.

"Okay, what's your plan big fella?"

*

It was beginning to get dark when Jed came from the tent where they had the group tied up; he joined his paw at the campfire.

"Paw that really smells good, let me get some of that grub your eating on," said Jed.

"You mean your hunger outweighs your need to smoke those weeds? It's been some time since we've had some moose; boy go on and get some it's mighty tasty." Jed cut some of the moose meat that was suspended above the fire.

"Them kids; what they in there doing besides bleeding?" Merle asked with a half smile.

"Their being still sitting down. I seen the one they call Hank has some fire in him, that's why you gave him the what for huh paw?" Jed asked. Merle was looking in a direction of sounds where twigs were being broken under foot. Merle pulled his gun pointing it in that direction. He seen it was Tabitha and holstered the gun. She entered the camp with Keith in the lead; his hands were tied in front of him. She had seen the two around the campfire and nudged Keith over towards them. Keith was scanning the area; he wondered where the pack was. The plan was to bring Keith back to the camp as if he was tied up and she pretended not to know about the murder. Then once he seen that everyone was okay, he'd free them and make a run for it while Tabitha had the drop on them. It probably wasn't the best plan, but it was all they could come up with in the short time they had, but if it worked they would be at her mercy. She could do whatever her revenge called for. Just the sight of Merle made her blood boil; she would forever view him in a different light.

"Put him in the small tent with the others," Merle said while standing.

"So far, so good," Keith said to himself. When Tabitha was almost past Merle leading Keith, Merle surprised them saying, "wait, hold up Tabby." They stopped; Merle walked up to Keith then punched him hard in his stomach. Keith folded over; the punch took the wind from him. Then he stood back up in pain staring hard at Merle face to face.

"Now he can be put with the rest of them, now they all have something in common; the pain to understand not to cross me. Run again boy, and I'll peel your skin from the bones. NOW GET!"

Tabitha grabbed Keith by his arm and led him away from Merle heading for the tent. Keith entered the tent and seen everyone, but Michael. They were tied and on the floor of the tent. Hank face was a bit swollen, but he was able to manage a smile when he seen Keith.

"Everyone she's with us; that man they killed was her real father. I'll explain everything once we are out of here," said Keith.

"Untie me so I can get my hands on Merle," said Hank.

"He's mine, y'all leave when you see the chance," said Tabitha.

"Have any of you seen Michael?" Amanda asked.

"That mean old man is gonna come in here and punish us again," said Beth louder then she intended.

"Shhhh! All of you shut your soup holes," said Tabitha then turned to Keith.

"You untie them and I'll take care of the wicked ones out there, it'll buy you some time and I'll catch up later." Then she took one step away from him, turned around, and flew into Keith's arms placing her lips on his.

Everyone, even Keith was surprised, but he found himself hugging and kissing her back. Then she tore herself away from him holding him at arm's length while looking him in his eyes saying, "for luck!" Suddenly, she left the tent; Keith was stunned, Hank was the closest to him so he kicked Keith's leg snapping him back to reality. Keith removed his rope that Tabitha had tied loose. Then he began to untie the others. Tabitha stepped from the tent; crickets could be heard along with other nightly sounds. The campfire was radiant illuminating the night as a full moon hung up in the sky. Both men were still over by the fire; she couldn't wait on Keith, and the others like her and Keith had planned. The revenge burned so hot inside of her you could light a cigarette on her forehead. She removed her bow and readied an arrow. It was getting even more difficult for her to even look at Merle. Both men looked up only to see Tabitha looking down an arrow at them.

"Whoa! Tabby stop playing around with that darn thing, what done got your panties in a bunch?" Jed asked.

"I know what y'all did to Clem; y'all killed him in cold blood," shouted Tabitha.

"Listen here Tabby, I was gonna tell you about your uncle trying to kill me Buck and Jed. I was just waiting on the right time to tell you. I know you and him were close, I know that you loved your uncle Clem so I understand why you must be upset now put that thing away and come give your father a hug, we'll get through this together," said Merle. Tabitha had tears flowing from her eyes.

"Stop lying to me! I know you killed him for the mineral rights; your greed for money got him killed. What you didn't know is that maw told me before she died that your brother Clem is my real father, now I'm gonna make you pay for what you did to him," said Tabitha with her face wet with tears and contorted from rage. Merle took a moment to soak this new information in.

"I knew them two were sweet on each other and figured years ago you were his. You look more like him than anyone. I never let your mother know because I knew Clem would leave whatever was his to his only child which is you. It's no big surprise about your maw and Clem. I'm no fool I seen the way they would look at each other. Me and the boys was gonna take your mineral rights nice like and leave you a little something, but now there is no more use in pretending. Knowing you are not my real daughter, I'll drop you where you stand. Point that thing elsewhere, I won't tell you again."

"I'm willing to take the chance, I believe I could place this arrow in your neck before you could get out the long barrel gun of yours," Tabitha said with confidence.

"That may be true, but what about Buck who is about thirty feet behind you with his sniper rifle trained at your pretty little head. You know me well enough to know that I don't bluff," Merle said with a sneer. She knew Buck could be a few feet from you and you wouldn't even know it. He had sniper training she wished he had taught her when she was younger. Tabitha felt a presence, and then slightly turned her head to see, only to be met with the butt end of Buck's rifle to the side of her head. She dropped to the ground like a rock. Merle and his sons now stood over her.

"I didn't bluff Tabby, but I did lie how close Buck was to you," Merle said with a wicked grin on his face. His words weren't received by Tabitha; the blow had knocked her out cold.

Chapter 16

Tabitha awoke looking at the ceiling and walls of a tent; to her surprise there was Keith, and the others she didn't know. They were still here in the tent and tied in worse than before. She along with the rest of them had been hog tied, on their sides bent in the touching the toe position with hands tied to their ankles. She had tied cattle and hog before, but never thought she'd ever be tied like this. Keith was at the opposite end of her.

"Tabitha, are you hurt?" Keith asked.

"Only my head and pride; I have this monster headache, I owe Buck for that. I thought you guys were freed. How did you get back into them there ropes?" Tabitha asked.

"Shortly after you walked out there, that Buck guy came in catching us off guard. We didn't even hear him come in. Anyway he held us at gunpoint and retied us. I guess that's when he came after you," answered Amanda.

"He's been known to be as quiet as church mice," Tabitha added.

"Tabitha, why didn't you stick to our plan?" Keith asked with a raised eyebrow.

"I'm sorry about that, my anger got the best of me; I just wanted to put some hurt on Merle. The more I think about it, I'm not sure the outcome would have been any different with Buck in the picture we didn't plan for him."

"After they brought you in I heard them say the first thing in the morning they're gonna drop us all down a mine shaft. That way if our bodies are ever found it would look like kids being careless and had a tragic accident," mentioned Hank.

"You got to admit that probably would be an open and shut case with the law. Tabitha, Keith brought us up to speed on everything so the way I see it them killing you along with us kills two birds with one stone, while making Merle and his brood of vipers rich," Mae added.

Beth begin to cry; in between her sobs she managed to say, "can't any of you see that we're gonna be dead in a matter of hours. I don't want to die."

"None of us wants to die Beth, you must hang in there and don't give up hope, we've made it this far by sticking together and fighting together, said Van with confidence.

The tent flaps came open; Michael appeared with his rock knife and spear in hand.

"Michael! You came back for us," said Amanda as he began to cut her loose.

"You know I couldn't leave you guys behind," he said with a smile.

"Hurry up will you, we have no time to waste," said Hank giving his best friend a look of thanks. Amanda seen his hands was swollen with bumps on them.

"Michael, what happened to your hands?" Amanda asked.

"Just a few stings, nothing serious, "he replied. Michael freed them all and led them away from camp to a place in the trees where they could still see the campfire.

"Why are we stopping here?"

"I need all of you to wait here, I must go back."

"We're free, why go back?" Amanda asked.

"They have our weapons and probably a cell phone, a radio, or something we can call for help. None of us have a phone remember," Michael explained.

"And let's keep in mind they have guns, we need to slow them down so we can get away. I'm coming with," Hank said with determination.

"Me too, he has my big knife, bow, and arrows, plus a neck I need to get my hands around," said Tabitha.

"Hank and I, we know each other's plays; no one else, no time to argue. I'll bring your weapons; all of you keep your heads down, eyes open, and mouths shut. You need to stay tuned in to that camp over there because if this goes south we need you guys hauling your butts up out of here."

"Didn't you and Hank teach us that there is strength in numbers? Maybe you two shouldn't go by yourselves," questioned Van.

Michael smiled before saying, "these people are crazed and they play for keeps, we have no room for error. Keep your eyes on that camp, I have the numbers on my side, I brought along some friends whose gonna help us out. Come on Hank I'll explain along the way." Then him and Hank disappeared in the night.

The three men in the big tent had settled down and went to sleep. Their serene setting was short-lived when the back of their tent lit up with bright orangish-red flames. The three awakened feeling the heat on their faces. They jumped to their feet grabbing their weapons, and then ran outside to the other tent that held Tabby and the youngins. When the three men hurried in the other tent this is what Hank and Michael were waiting for, the two scouts sneaked behind them just to the doorway and removed the string that had the bag tied to a stick and held the bag shut, then tossed it inside the tent. Both scouts closed the tent flaps and tied them shut so no one could get out, then ran to be with the others. Merle, Buck, and Jed noticed cut rope on the tent's floor, the kids had escaped. What was seen next was a plastic bag the size of a basketball landing at their feet. All three men heard the sound of a furious swarm of insects coming out from the bag by the hundreds.

"Wasps!" Merle shouted. The flying stab stingers were relentless in their attack. The men panicked knocking each other around just to get out. Meanwhile, Michael and Hank hurried in the tent that was partially on fire grabbing their knives, the bow, and arrows, but didn't see any communication device of any kind. Screams could be heard from the men being stung. Michael and Hank made it back to the rest of the group who had their eyes glued on the camp. The tent being on fire illuminated a small area around the camp. Painful screams of Merle, Buck, and Jed reached their ears. The two scouts told them how they had released the hornets in the tent. Tabby knew these three men were feeling the wrath of nature she suddenly gave way to insane laughter.

Chapter 17

The group had traveled for a couple of hours; the sun was coming up over the horizon when Beth insisted they allow her to rest. Everyone took the opportunity to take the load off their feet. Keith introduced Tabitha to the group. After everyone told her their names her reply was, "y'all can call me Tabby," She went on to say, "there is a Ranger station near bouts, our best chance would be to head there even if no one is there they might have a radio."

"Tabby, would there be any form of transportation there?" Michael asked.

"The Rangers mostly came this far in on horse. Merle and my paw would ride as all out here in the truck. Two would ride up front while the rest of us would ride in the back bed of the truck. We would ride so far then hike the rest of the way in. Been doing it that way for years, so if your looking for a motor vehicle of any kind the chances are very slim so you city folk step aside and let me do what I do."

She then stood then went and climbed one of the nearby trees; they watched her go up and could hardly believe Tabby's ability to climb like an animal.

"She's a tomboy," Keith said proudly, smiling, and keeping his eyes on her.

"What is she doing?" Mae asked.

"My guess is she's getting her bearings," answered Hank as he put his arms around her.

"What happened to that shy, bashful young man I started out on this trip with?" Mae asked giving him her best smile.

"Let's just say I've embraced you in my heart and my heart has been waiting for me to catch up to it."

"That's so sweet come here you!" Mae said then Hank planted his lips on hers. Michael saw the way Amanda was watching Mae and Hank realizing they all had been through hell and hadn't even found help yet. Him and Amanda barely had time to even be close to each other for a long period of time. Michael walked up behind her, turned her slowly around facing him, and took her into his arms passionately kissing her. Keith, Beth, and Van were still watching Tabby in the tree. When she came down all eyes were on her with hopes of some good news. Tabby pointed her finger in the direction they needed to go.

"I can see the Rangers outpost; it's about a mile that way."

"That's good right?" Beth asked with raised eyebrows.

"Yes, it has to be; we haven't had such luck since this whole nightmare started," answered Van.

"Let's just say for now it's a good sign," replied Tabby. Keith noticed Tabby looked a bit disturbed.

"What do you mean for now?"

"Yeah, what's the mystery? What aren't you telling me?" Michael asked.

"I looked on our back trail and didn't see anyone following us, but there is a lot of tree cover that makes it hard to see the ground," Tabby informed them.

"Again, that's good right? You not seeing anyone is good right?" Beth interpreted.

"That's what got me on edge. Although, I can't see anyone I have a feeling we are being followed. Like it or not Merle and his sons' will come at us with everything they've got now that y'all have beat them. We need to move with the quickness at one speed as fast as we can until we reach that Ranger's outpost. No resting; no stopping for anything."

"You all heard Tabby. We must get to that outpost if we are to have any chance of rescue. I know we are all tired and beat up, but this is when we need to dig deep to survive. Once we start running if anyone must rest, rest on your feet as you run. That's all I got. Michael, do you have anything?" Hank asked.

"I don't have much; Hank has pretty much said it all. Just remember to stay together. There are eight of us so we can run in line two by two helping and encouraging each other to keep up. Tabby knows the way so it will be her and Keith in the lead and me and Amanda will bring up the rear making sure no one falls behind," said Michael.

"Can we go now? Enough of this bumping our gums; let's go!" Tabby said as she took off pulling Keith by his arm alongside of her. The rest followed in behind and the run proved to be difficult with obstacles going over and or around boulders along the way. It was with fallen, dead trees, thrones that pricked their ankles and legs, low, hanging tree limbs with leaves smacking them in their faces; some mossy wet areas slowing their steps; roots partially exposed causing some to trip and fall; running into spider webs, and hanging vines. The group kept moving not to be defeated by the obstacles they encountered from the dense growth of trees. Finally, Tabby led them into a circled clearing; everyone stopped to catch their breath.

"Tabby, where is the outpost?" Keith asked. She pointed upward then they seen it; suspended up was several large logs about twenty feet high supporting a small Ranger outpost. It looked like a miniature log cabin. They all marveled at the height of it, but was more so overjoyed to see something that man had made which meant people were here or not far from here.

"Wow, this would have been easy to miss. From a casual glance the logs that support this outpost looks like the rest of the trees," Michael commented.

"I've never seen anything like it," Hank added.

"How do we get up there?" Keith asked.

"There is a rope ladder hanging by the center supporting log," answered Tabby.

"How did you know about the ladder?" Van asked.

"Because where I stand I can see it silly. No more questions let's get up there," said Tabby taking the lead. The ladder went up to a hatched door in the floor of the outpost. Once all was inside they took a look around. There was a couple of cots for sleeping, a desk with a chair, and over the desk was a large map of the area. Also, in the cabin was a first aid kit, fire extinguisher, several flares, two flash lights, small wood burning stove with a coffee pot on it, a small wall hanging mirror, several rolls of toilet tissue, and two basin's for potty relief. The four-sided outpost had a window on each wall for looking in every direction. Some were at the windows looking at the breath-taking beauty of things from this high up.

"Tabby, why was this thing built up so high?" Keith asked.

"Maybe to give the Rangers a bird's eye view big fella,"

"How do they travel to and from here? I don't see any vehicles," Amanda asked.

"Horseback, I doubted if anyone would be here. This is mostly used for emergencies like bad weather, medical aid, regrouping, and all sorts of stuff," Tabby said.

"I think it's safe to say we classify as an emergency," Mae replied.

"I'm gonna backtrack and cover any tracks we made and hope to throw them off of our trail."

"Tabby you think they could find us with all that wilderness out there?" Hank asked.

"It's possible; what we have is our favor is they don't know anything about this place. You see Merle assigned us all a part of this land to hunt and this was my area for five miles around. Now if I don't go and cover our tracks it will lead him right to here; there is no Rangers here and by the looks of the dust build up no one has been here in some time. Buck was a sniper in the service; he's the best when it comes to shooting and hunting. I'm good, but he's great he taught me so I'm gone get and should be back in the morning. Y'all get some wood up here before it gets too dark."

"Then a few of us can come with you and make sure you make it back safe," said Keith. She walked up to Keith, "that's sweet big fella, but y'all would just slow me down. I'll be back soon enough." Tabby then kissed Keith on his forehead, opened the hatch and headed down the rope ladder. Keith, Hank, and Michael followed her down. She ran through the brush and they started to collect wood. The wood burning stove provided heat without lighting up their position. The big map of the area was the center of everyone's attention. Judging from the map's scale it showed a river two miles south of them, some woods, barren land, and some mountains. What really stood out was what looked to be a highway about eleven miles west of their position. This brought a ray of hope among them.

"Can we all agree to head for that highway at the first sign of light in the morning?" Michael asked.

"I don't want to rain on anyone's parade but, I think if we stay here overnight we may not ever see that highway," answered Van.

"Yes, your good with history and statistics, but we all need to talk about this," said Hank.

"I say we take what we need and take our chances roughing it through the night to get to that highway," answered Van.

"We also run the risk of something that may want to eat us if we travel at night," said Mae with conviction.

"She has a good point," Hank added.

"I can't stand this waiting around for those deranged maniacs to come and kill us. Let's go Van," said Beth.

"I'm in agreement with Mae; no telling what's out there and worse yet, we wouldn't be able to see what's coming at us," said Amanda and Michael chimed in.

"I'm torn both ways; on one hand I want to keep it moving before Merle and his brood catch up to us. On the other hand, I don't want to face any nocturnal creatures that want to rip me apart. All things considered I lean to the side of caution; I say let's play it safe and wait it out," said Michael.

"It's a no brainer to me. Tabby asked us to wait on her and that's exactly what I'm gonna do," Keith replied.

"I say we go; how do you know she's not in league with those crazed men?"

"Because she saved my life from a raging river Beth and that's good enough for me. For our sake I pray she's in one piece to help us out of here. They killed her dad; she can be trusted," Keith retorted.

"Let's put it to a vote; we are still a pack and the majority rules. Who all want to chance going for the highway tonight raise their hands? Who all want to chance staying till morning touch their nose with one finger," Michael instructed. Beth and Van were the only two to raise their hands; the rest had one finger to their nose.

"Looks like we wait until first light," said Michael.

"I'm scared and I'm tired of being passive letting all of you make the decisions when my life is on the line. Van we can make it together without them. Will you come with me?" Beth asked.

"Come on, don't do this. We all have gotten this far; play it smart. Don't dummy up on us now we're almost out of this mess. You know the old saying; don't change strokes in the middle of the river," Hank reasoned.

"Sorry guys, but I have to agree with Beth and must agree to disagree with the rest of you. I'm familiar with how to follow a map; we just head west for about eleven miles to the highway. Please don't try to stop us; Beth and I are gonna go and if anyone wants to join us we welcome them." It was clear there was no changing Van and Beth's mind so since they couldn't talk them out of going they did the next best thing. They equipped them with supplies to better their chances and also armed Van with a knife as Beth had the spear. They all went outside to see the two off. Everyone hugged and wished each other well and watched Van and Beth leave and some had tears in their eyes. Once secure back in the outpost Amanda asked Mae, "so you think they will make it?"

"Girl, I hope so, but we both know they stood a better chance with us. We have run and you and I who are two beautiful females, one strong bully, two awesome scouts, and a female Tarzan out there somewhere.

Chapter 18

The air had a chill in it and an almost full moon was casting its reflective light on the land. Beth and Van were thankful for the moon because it provided some guidance. Van was telling her as long as they kept the moon slightly to their left it would maintain a good course for the highway. After traveling seven miles, the two had tired walking at a fast pace for the first couple of miles as fast as the wooded area would allow them to go. The lack of nutrition and rest was beginning to take the toll. Now fatigue had set in and their walk slowed. Both were weary stumbling hap-hazard as if they were drunk.

"Why don't you two take a load off your feet and stay with us for a spell," came a voice from the dark. The two stopped tensing up from whoever this was out there. Beth grabbed the spear sticking it out before her, turning around slowly trying to see where this voice was coming from. Van was doing the same with the knife outreached with one hand, and the other hand balled into a fist.

"Drop the crude weapons, we have guns," came the voice. Beth was so scared her fingers wouldn't open to drop the spear. Hard as Van and Beth tried they couldn't see who this was lurking out there. It didn't sound like Merle so who could it be?

"I won't ask you again," the voice came again.

"Beth run!" Van grabbed her hand taking off running as fast as he could with Beth in tow. They made it twenty yards when Beth felt something wet and warm splash across her face, it was blood she could taste it in her mouth. Van went to the ground pulling her with him. They both fell rolling on their backs. Although, the moonlight was dim it was light enough for her to see the red growing circle on Van's shoulder; Van had been shot. He grabbed his shoulder wincing from the pain while sucking air through his clenched teeth. She stood to her feet fast and attempted pulling Van to his feet. The three men came from the dark of the trees that concealed them. She let go of Van's hand and backed away from the men a couple of steps with her spear pointed towards them. Then she thought better of running and stopped to wait on Van; she just couldn't leave him like this. Van struggled getting to his feet, all the while concealing his knife up his sleeve with his good hand. Now the three men were close enough to see the faces of Merle, Jed, and Buck. All of them looked different with their faces and necks swollen. Jed looked the worse, with one of his eyes swollen shut that he had to constantly wipe with the back of his sleeve due to it draining.

"Darn right purdy ain't we? Them hornets your friends released on us did a job on me and my boys. Jed here got stung, but his one eye got it bad, didn't have enough sense to cover them. Doubt if he'll ever see out of that eye again. You youngins are the blame for that and must be punished," said Merle standing with both arms crossed. Van was standing with his wounded arm hanging at his side. The distance between his and merle was about ten feet. Van thought to himself, "I'm probably gonna bleed out from this gunshot wound and die; if I can get close enough to Merle I can stab him with this knife to buy Beth some time to get away." Van let the knife slip from his sleeve into his hand and west at Merle with the remaining strength he had left bringing the knife high over head in hand, and his one good arm to plant it in Merle's chest. A shot rang out hitting Van in the back and he fell to the ground dying with his eyes open while still clenching the knife in hand. Merle never moved; he looked down on the young man with a smile. Buck had his rifle across his back with a silencer on it that he used to shoot Van in his shoulder, the .45 seal auto in his hand in what ended Van's life. Beth screamed loudly and snapped, charging at Buck with the intent of running him through with her spear. He side stepped her punching Beth in her jaw, she went down hard dropping her spear then tried to get up only to be met by Buck's boot to her forehead. She lay there unconscious as blood came from her mouth.

*

Tabby was proud of herself for having done each a good job of cleaning up their back trail. Her mind drifted off back to the times she shared with her mother Louise when she was alive. Louise would always impart words of wisdom that didn't make a lot of sense at the time. Stuff like, "each tub must sit on its own bottom or I won't fatten frogs for snakes." It wasn't until Tabby would experience life adversities that gave her mother's words true meaning. Tabby's favorite she heard was, "you can see farther through a tear then a telescope." The tears she was leaking through now made her see rage and revenge; destroying Merle was the only way to stop the pain. Another saying came to mind, "if you go for revenge dig two graves,"

Tabby didn't care if she did die in the process. The loss of her mother and the murder of her father was a bit too much to handle so she had herself a good cry. Tears were streaming down her face as she let it all loose along with sighs and sniffles. The sound of a gunshot reached her ears bringing her out of it. She wiped her face with the sleeve of her jacket, readied herself, and then jumped from the tree she was resting in. She ran in the direction she heard the shot from only to be confronted by a lone wolf. She stopped in her tracks. It growled showing its deadly teeth. The distance was less than seven yards from her. Tabby didn't have time to bring her bow to bear on this thing so she grabbed for her long knife on her hip hoping there wasn't any more of them. The wolf slowly came forward low as though it was ready to pounce. She let the knife fly from her hand, it buried to the hit in the animal's chest before it could leap from the ground. The wolf lay there on its side with the tongue hanging out. Tabby west to the wolf, removed her knife and wiped the blood from it on the K-9's fur then put the knife back on her hip and took no time running towards the sound of the gunshot.

*

Although, they were suspended twenty feet above the forest floor and in a cable outpost some of the group was able to fall asleep. Thoughts of not being too far from the highway and just knowing that crazed men were out there somewhere looking for them made no one want to close their eyes. The two couples were cuddled up in the blankets against opposite walls. Keith was going from window to window at times. Being on the lookout, but more so with hopes of seeing Tabby return safe. He was smitten with love when it came to her. It was something he couldn't explain; all he knew is that she weighed heavy on his mind. Something occurred to Keith; he stopped pacing from window to window and said, "I know I'm not the brightest bulb among you, but I've been giving something some thought. Shouldn't we assume the worst case scenario that we will be found up here by Merle and his bunch? And if so there is only one way out of here." What Keith said made sense. If they were discovered this cabin would be a deathtrap. Hopefully, they would make it to morning, being up high, and the location wasn't easy to spot. First sign of daylight they would leave, but the thought of what Keith said sunk in. No one would even attempt to get any sleep now.

Chapter 19

Beth was awakened with a few slaps to her face. Her hands were tied so tight she barely had any feelings in them. She was in a sitting position leaned against a tree.

"I'll only ask you this question once. If you don't answer me I'll take pleasure in using this knife I have on my hip here to cut your pretty little lips off. Can you show me where the others are?" Merle asked and she just nodded yes.

Jed went over and pulled Beth by her hair standing her on her feet.

"Lead the way heifer, don't be stupid and try to run. I'll shoot you, I'm bitter, you and your friends caused me to lose my eye so I can't wait to hurt somebody, anybody. Don't let that be you," said Jed. Beth didn't remember exactly the way she came, but did remember most of the way and to keep the moon on her opposite side from which she came.

"Poor Van," she thought to herself. "He got killed trying to help me." They traveled some distance with Jed pushing Beth roughly at times. She was so tired, but they wouldn't allow her to stop and rest after a few miles more of leading the men Beth stopped.

Merle went forward, stood over her, and drew his hand back to slap back for stopping. She covered her face for the coming blow saying, "up there," she said while pointing. Merle stopped his arm mid-air from coming in contact with her.

"What did you say?" Merle asked. Beth began to cry again, but pointed upward with both of her tied hands. All of the men looked up. It took a moment, but they seen it. Buck brought his rifle to bare looking through his scope at the window of the outpost.

"Well I'll be," said Buck.

"Look at that there paw," Jed added.

"I'd heard tale years back they were gonna build this Rangers outpost out here somewhere near bouts, but I never thought they'd carry it through, "said Merle.

"Paw what if we run into any Rangers; can I treat them as hostels?"

"Yeah boy you take them out and that goes for you too Jed. The whole lot of them must go. No one and nothing will stop me from getting what I want. Just remember Tabby is the only one we need alive long enough to sign over the mineral rights to me so don't either of you clowns kill her yet," said Merle.

Jed grabbed Beth by her hair.

"Paw, what should I do with this one?"

"Just hold on to her, let's see how bad they want her back," said Merle, then he cupped his hands to his mouth.

"Hey, you up there, come down or we'll commence to shooting," no answer came.

"Buck, put a round through that window up there," Merle instructed. Buck put one round through the window and it shattered alarming a squirrel to scurry from a nearby tree. No one came out.

"Last chance, we got some coal all with us, come down or get burned down," Merle commanded, but still nothing.

"Paw, if we burn this thing down, wouldn't it kill Tabby? You told us to keep her alive," said Jed.

"Trust me boy, people will do what they must to haul butts away from fire. I don't care how high they are up they'll jump. We don't care if she jumps and breaks her legs we just need her to be able to sign this paper I have folded here in my pocket," replied Merle.

"Please can I go now, I've showed you what you want," asked Beth.

"Hold tight little missy, we haven't got your friends yet. Buck, splash some oil on them there support poles and light them up, "said Merle. Buck did as he was told and in no time the oil and sap from the timber fueled the fire making it grow traveling upwards to the outpost brightening up the surrounding area. Suddenly, the entire cabin became engulfed in flames. No one had screamed and no one had jumped so it was then Merle knew no one was in there.

*

There was an uneasy feel in the cabin; although they had shelter and was high off the ground they still felt trapped. All agreed to sleep outside a safe distance from the outpost to play it safe. Just when the group is a little more at ease in the dark of the woods, they hear glass from the window break. It was time to get far away from here as possible. The group ran in the direction they figured to be towards the highway. When the forest lit up all was compelled to stop and look back, the cabin was up in flames. Thoughts crossed their minds that they could have still been in there.

"We must keep moving," said Hank. As they turned to leave a metallic sound was heard like a spring was sprung; then came a blood curdling scream. It was Mae; she stepped in an animal's trap. The manmade metal jaws were clamped tight on her lower leg. No doubt her scream was heard by Merle and his crew. Amanda went by Mae's side to hold her up as Michael and Hank immediately held the jaws of the trap open. Then Keith lifted her leg from it. Mae sat there on the ground moaning while holding her bleeding leg, the pain was excruciating.

"How did something like this get out here?" Keith asked.

"Who cares how it got out here, our concern should be for her," Hank replied.

"I'm sorry you all I didn't mean it like that," said Keith.

"I know and I apologize. I'm a bit uptight; I just need to put some hurt on who hurt my girl, "Hank reasoned.

"I say Merle put this trap and maybe some more out here as his plan B to slow us down," replied Michael.

Hank gave Mae a small stick to bite down on then tore the lower part of his shirt wrapping it around her leg.

"Their gonna be coming after us, can you stand?" Hank asked, but she didn't answer.

Hank asked her again, "Mae can you stand?" Through pain with squinted eyes she nodded her head yes, then went to stand, and stumbled a bit. Amanda and Hank helped by supporting both of her arms. Mae limped on it trying not to apply all of her weight on it, she favored the leg. The group was on the move again, at a slower pace being cautious of their footing.

"I don't think it's broken, but it's gonna leave a hell-of-ah-scar," said Mae managing to give Hank a weak smile. She prayed a silent prayer that no one would get hurt or killed because in her current condition she could no longer keep up.

*

The three men ran in the direction of the scream with Beth in tow. Buck used his tracking skills; it was easy to see the youngster's tracks. Buck could tell they were running due to the increase of spaces apart of the tracks they left behind. He stopped and held up one of his sprung traps his paw had told him to place around out here. It was apparent the trap had blood stains. The three men smiled displaying tobacco stained teeth.

Chapter 20

The youngsters tracks had went in a couple different directions. Merle, Buck, and Jed knew the kids had to be close so they split up and spread out to cover more ground. The youngsters went separate way, Jed was getting frustrated; he had lost an eye, body had been stung multiple times, was also hungry and tired.

"I could be somewhere enjoying me some bud, but these interloping kids ruined everything," Jed said allowing himself to stop under a tree taking a good look around. He felt something hit his face; it was wet, then another drip. Jed took his hand and wiped his face. When he looked to see what it was he seen it was red, than put it to his nose to smell. Blood! Jed quickly looked up, but couldn't really make out the form, but he knew it to be human. The group had decided Mae would be safer in a tree. No way could she keep up with her injury so they helped her up in the tree. No one liked the idea of leaving her up in a tree, but it made sense to hide her because with Mae's current condition she could walk slow, but couldn't run. The group decided they must lead them away from her. It was Mae's idea to stay behind; she would not allow anyone to get hurt on the count of her. Hank was adamant on remaining behind with her to help if she needed him. Mae wouldn't hear of it. She told him and the group as long as she was up in the tree out of sight she would be safe, and she figured the group would need him more. Amanda insisted on staying with her so Hank didn't want to argue with Amanda or Mae on the matter. He reluctantly went along with the others to lead Merle and his son's away from the tree Amanda and Mae were in to save her life along with theirs, because leaving her behind was out of the question. For now they had to do what must be done. The girls in the tree knew he had seen them since he was aiming his rifle up in their general direction. Each girl held on to the tree tight. Jed fired a shot that missed them both, but it was close enough to Mae's face that it caused splinters of weed to fly in her cheek and neck. She let out a cry and fell to the ground. Jed walked a couple steps, stood over her letting his rifle hang to his back with the strap across his chest. Then he pulled his knife with the look of a person with a blood lust. Mae was trying to get to her feet when she seen Jed lift his knife to end her life. Mae put up both of her hands in defense," no! Please don't!" Mae pleaded with the man holding the knife. Suddenly from the tree, gravity helped one hundred and ten pounds of Amanda to come down hard on Jed causing him to slam on his back and release the knife from his hand. Amanda lay there a bit dazed trying to clear her head. Mae seen Jed recovering, but Amanda wasn't getting up fast enough to be that close to him. Mae found the strength to limp over to Jed, straddle him by sitting on his chest taking her fist, and started raining blow after blow down on his face of the man who had attempted to kill them. She hit him so hard it knocked a tooth from his mouth. Jed punched Mae in the stomach causing her to double over then he back-hand slapped her. The force of the blow caused her to go rolling to the side of him. He crawled over grabbing the knife when Amanda jumped on his back. He rolled her over on her back bringing the knife up and down. She caught and held his wrist back with both hands trying to prevent the knife from doing damage. He was too strong; Jed felt her beginning to weaken then broke her grip on his wrist. The knife pierced Amanda's stomach and she screamed.

Mae also screamed "no!" Jed stood with his bloody knife in hand, grabbed Mae by her throat then lifted her with one hand until her back was against the tree. Mae scratched at his arm that was holding her, but it did no good. Jed held Mae looking her in the eyes as he brought the knife up to stab Mae in her chest. She tried to scream, but couldn't because of the grip he had on her neck. She closed her eyes praying a fervent prayer. Jed's whole body did a sudden jerk and went stiff dropping Mae to the ground. She coughed trying to regain her breath. Mae looked up and seen it; an arrow protruded from his stomach as he failed in his attempt to pull it from his back. Jed stumbled and fell to the ground. Tabby came running into view with her bow in hand with another arrow ready to fly. She checked Jed's body for a pulse. It was plain to see he was dead. Tabby helped Mae to her feet then Mae limped to Jed's dead form and kicked him. Both women went over to Amanda; her breathing was labored. She was laying flat on her back with her hand on her wound.

"Does it look as bad as it feels?" Amanda asked wincing, looking up at Tabby as she was inspecting the knife wound. Mae sat there on the ground beside her friend Amanda; she didn't like seeing Amanda like this.

"Hard to say; if the blade didn't come in contact with any internal organs you could make it, but in order to do that we need to cut some strips of our clothes to make some compression bandages to stop you from bleeding," answered Tabby. Mae and, Tabby worked fast making something to help save Amanda; as her and Tabby was ripping fabric, Mae's eyes had tears coming from them she felt the need to say, "Amanda, thank you for helping me and I'm sorry I couldn't prevent this from happening to you."

"Girl, there was nothing you could do. Thank me by drying your eyes and patching me up," said Amanda with a weak smile. By the time they had finished Amanda's stomach was wrapped tight. She was weak from losing so much blood and started to fade from consciousness.

*

He knew it wouldn't be long now because it was only so far a person could run to out this way. If the tracks kept going the way they were headed the youngsters would fall off this rugged cliff that was nearby. Buck knew he had to be near to those he tracked; he felt it on instinct alone. It was a gut feeling that had saved his life in the past more than once over sea's in war. He walked with caution; his sniper rifle at the ready. Buck noticed the three set of tracks he was following changed from three; now it was only two. He stood from looking down at the tracks knowing he had been out thought by some young boys, but it was too late, ambush! Buck pivoted around to a big bush that seemed to be the only place in this area of concealment. He seen through the foliage of the bush; there sat some gym shoes. Maybe these boys weren't as smart as he gave them credit for. One of them did a poor job of hiding. Buck fired into the bush he seen the shoes through. The silenced rifle made a sound as if it coughed three times; the short burst in the bush caused some birds to take flight from their roost. Then Buck made his way over to the bush only to find a set of gym shoes there with no one in them. Without warning from the dry leaves, a leg kicked out connecting with Buck's right knee bringing him down one way with the rifle slung from his hand the other. Michael, Keith, and Hank made up their minds to make a trap of their own. Michael's shoes would be used to distract their pursuers while Michael laid in wait under the leaves. The plan was for Michael to catch whoever was after them off guard, and the others would come to subdue them with overwhelming force. After bringing him down, Michael moved fast to gain top control with Buck, but Buck was fast and strong coupled with his military training made him a force to be reckoned with. Keith and Hank had to remain a good distance away in order for this to work with Michael surprising him. Buck managed to get to his feet. Both men squared off into fighting stances. Although, Buck had hornet stings on his face, Michael could still see the expression of a sinister smirk he had on his face, then Buck said, "I'm really gonna enjoy this." Buck threw a jab at Michael's face and Michael blocked it, but this was just to setup Buck's combination of the right cross that landed solid against Michael's head causing him to go down on his side. Buck lifted his feet to stomp the downed man only to be bull-dozed flat on his back with Keith on top. Buck felt like a professional line hacker ran into him whoever this kid was he had strength, but Buck was in good shape and had taken down bigger in his day. Buck brought his knee up hard into Keith's side making Keith clutch for his ribs. Before Buck completely stood Hank put a running flying knee to the side of Buck's head. He went down catching himself with one hand from hitting the ground then sprung back to his feet into a fighting stance only to turn and found himself facing Hank, Michael, and Keith coming at him straight on full speed.

*

"Amanda, we need to get away from here, we're gonna try to move you is that okay?" Mae asked.

"Yeah, yeah I just feel so tired, just let me lay here awhile longer," Amanda answered batting her eyes slowly.

"Listen girlfriend we are still in danger so we must haul our butts out of here so please Amanda summon whatever strength you have left and let's move," Mae said loudly with Tabby on alert to shoot another arrow at the first sign of trouble.

"Our best chance is to get with the others. I spied them when I came looking for you. They're not far away, come on Amanda. Mae and I will help you to walk," Tabby insisted. They walked several yards and Tabby felt she had to say, "you girls know if anything jumps out at us I won't be able to get an arrow in my bow in time."

"Why…would…something come at us Tabby?" Amanda asked.

"Because your ringing the diner bell with that red stuff leaking from you." Hearing her say that brought the dreadful memory to Amanda and Mae of how the bus driver died.

*

Merle was looking over the cliff when he heard a shot fired from somewhere nearby. He turned his attention from the cliff and ran almost dragging Beth in the direction he believed the shot came from. After coming through the thicket there to his right down the hill a ways was a bear; it was chowing down on some berries. Merle wanted to shoot him right there on the spot, but he didn't want to alert anyone that he was nearby so given the nature of Merle he just picked up a big rock and threw it hard as he could at the bear. It connected hitting the bear on his snout; it spotted Merle and Beth then bellowed out a loud roar. Merle laughed knowing the bear couldn't get to him up here. The massive beast sniffed the air catching their scent and made an attempt to get to these humans who had brought it out of its moment of peace. Merle wasted no time putting distance between him and the bear. He ran as fast as he could still pulling Beth along. He was pulling her so hard she felt as though her arm was coming out of the socket.

*

Buck weighed the odds even with his skills one of these three might get a lucky punch in causing him to be overtaken by them all. His motto was to fight smarter not harder. Buck ran back through the dense trees to better his chances. He was glad to see they were coming after him instead of going to find his rifle back there. Once he disposed of these three he would go back to retrieve it. Buck darted in between trees causing Michael, Keith, and Hank to split up in order not to attack all at once. Hank was the closest on his heels; Buck ducked behind a tree using his warfare tactics and to wait for the right moment here behind this tree. Hank knew he seen Buck run somewhere around this way. Hank stopped when he seen the cliff then turned around into a big fist. Spit flew from Hank's mouth followed by Buck kicking him in his mid-section. Michael and Keith were there in time for Keith to kick Buck in the back of his knee bringing him off balance as Michael followed through with a kick to Buck's chest making him go down when he was on one knee preparing to stand Hank was there to throw a kick. Buck caught his foot, but Hank was fast enough to hop up with his other foot, and kick Buck in his jaw. Buck wouldn't stay down; he stood reaching for his knife he carried on his hip only to find that it wasn't there.

"Looking for this?" Keith asked holding up the shiny blade then Keith went at Buck with it. Buck did some quick martial art move with his hands disarming Keith then caught the knife before it hit the ground. The two scouts and Keith brought their knives out. Buck threw his knife and it found its way into Keith's thigh. He went down hollering, but knew better of removing the knife for fear of bleeding to death. Hank and Michael charged him with everything they had, every knife thrust, kick, and punch they threw at Buck he blocked them all. Then Buck was able to throw some punches and kicks of his own. He was effectively downing both scouts. Hank was bleeding from his mouth and Michael had blood coming from his nose with a fractured arm; Buck continued his assault.

Chapter 21

Buck was unaware of Mae, Amanda, and Tabby watching through the vegetation.

"Wait here girls," said Tabby making her way towards the fighting men. Buck was getting the best of Michael and Hank. Every time one of them would attempt to throw a peach or kick Buck would answer them connecting with brutal accuracy. Buck could have ended their lives, but enjoyed the beat down he was giving them like a cat plays with a mouse just before he eats it. Keith went for Buck considerably slower with his movements with the knife still embedded in his thigh. Buck seen him coming and did a roundhouse kick to Keith's face that sent him sliding back on his butt. Buck pointed at Keith saying, "you wait your turn." Then he turned grabbing Hank and Michael by their necks, lifted them up, then choke slammed them to the ground. Tabby appeared by Keith noticing the knife in his leg. She bent over and kissed Keith on the forehead.

"You stay put big fella." She stood then said loudly to Buck, "hey buck-ah-roo, pick on somebody your own size." Buck turned his attention away from the scouts who he knew wouldn't be getting up soon.

"Tabby, step away from that boy and come back with family. I won't ask you a second time," commanded Buck.

"Why don't you step away from them and come over here to say that to my face," said Amanda.

"Sure, why not, but if you make me come over there don't blame me if I bust you up a bit, and don't try to put an arrow in me. I'll shoot you before you can string an arrow in that darn thing. Throw it away from you slowly." She did as she was told, tossed the bow and arrow, but Tabby knew she couldn't beat Buck at hand to hand combat. Much of the stuff she knew he had taught her, but she knew she could out think him. She waited for him to come within range then quickly grabbed her Tarzan knife from its sheath on her hip throwing it at Buck's chest. Buck did the unexpected, he caught Tabby's blade from the air and with equal speed threw it back at her with force. The knife flew through the air fast, planting itself to the right of Tabby's chest, just under the shoulder propelling her back. She landed on her back next to Keith. Buck was surprised when he felt himself getting blows to the back of his head from Hank and Michael. With the remaining strength they had wasn't enough to hurt Buck, he turned slapping both scouts down. Thinking how boring this had become so he would end these two. This was the chance Tabby needed for him to take his eyes from her if only for a moment. Just when he was going to bend down and snap Michael and Hank's neck, Tabby said, "hey gung ho military man let's try that again." Buck turned and seen Tabby standing. She had taken the knife out and was bleeding from the knife wound in her chest.

"This won't end well for you Tabby. I've been ordered not to kill you, but I can slice you up little girl with that there knife of yours," warned Buck.

"Let's see about that," said Tabby throwing the knife he seen in her hand. Buck caught the knife as before, and then realized his fatal mistake in neglecting to see that she was holding two knives. Tabby had removed the knife from Keith's thigh and threw this knife alone with hers at the same time. Buck made some choking sounds from the instrument of death that was buried in his throat. He pulled from his neck and tried to walk, but staggered over by Tabby then fall at her feet never to move on his own again. Minutes later Amanda, Mae, Tabby, Keith, Hank, and Michael sat there in a clearing banged up, doing what they could to patch each other up. Michael and Hank looked badly wrapped up with torn rags from each other clothes', but for some the bleeding wouldn't stop. They all were in need of medical attention. Each were coupled up, all had more concerns about Amanda because she got it the worst and had lost much blood.

"How cute seeing all of you together like this," They all turned to see Merle holding Beth by her hair. Tabby was in a sitting position looking at this man she had lost all respect for.

"Merle it was all of bunch of lies huh? I mean with your love and concern for my well being and all."

"Tabby don't talk that self-righteous crap to me. You knew I wasn't your father, and we both know about your mother and my brother. Look pumpkin."

"Don't call me that, you don't have that right, "yelled Tabby.

"Fair enough, look Tabby I don't give a rat's behind about you being my brother's kid or that you killed Buck who I see on the ground over there. He was a tough one though, so I will assume Jed is dead as well. Call me cold-hearted, but I don't give two whoops about them either. I just want you to sign this paper I have here giving me ownership to the rights; I'll let you all go. Even this girl I got here so what do you say Tabby?" Beth was crying, but managed to say in between sobs, "he killed Van; shot him in the back in cold blood. Don't give this monster anything." Merle pulled his gun out and put it to Beth's temple.

"I'll kill her and then the rest of you one by one until you agree to my terms Tabby."

"Listen you twisted human being, many people have died over your greed. You won't get away with killing any of us. You are wicked and God will deal with the wicked," said Hank. Merle removed the gun from Beth's head and aimed it at Hank's genitals.

"Shut up before I change you from a rooster to a hen, snarled Merle then put his gun to Beth's chest.

"Don't do it Tabby, he's gonna kill us all anyway," Beth said. Merle cocked the hammer.

"Okay, okay I'll sign you can have the rights. Just let her go and leave us alone," Tabby pleaded.

"No! He can't have his way," shouted Beth turning, digging her nails deep across Merle's cheek. Out of rage and anger he shot her. There was a mixture of screams and sighs from the group, then everyone slowly stood looking behind Merle as he felt on his face assessing how deep her nails had went into his face. It was four long furrows that went down his cheek exposing raw skin. Beth lay at his feet breathing hard. Merle lifted his gun at the group. They looked wide-eyed in horror, but it wasn't the gun being aimed at them that brought about such fear. Merle's mistake was thinking he had installed that much fright in them. The massive brute of a bear had remembered Merle's scent and tracked him there. Now it stood behind him, towering over this man that had taunted it. The beast bellowed out a roar that made Merle soil himself. When he turned to shoot the bear it was too late. The bear hit Merle lifting him from his feet, slamming him into a nearby tree breaking many bones in his body. If that wasn't enough, the brute went over where Merle laid and bit a plug from his shoulder. Merle screamed, but couldn't move. The group wanted to run, but thought better of it knowing this would make the bear chase them. Suddenly from behind them they hear several voices shout, "get down!" The group didn't have to be told twice; they all dropped down then looked to see who was behind them. Everyone smiled with tears of joy to see all types of uniforms, park rangers, state police, paramedics, and a sheriff with deputies. It seemed like every law enforcement and first responder department in American was there. All of the law enforcement fire arms discharged all at once. The bear roared as the hot lead tore through its hide; it attempted to run at the shooters, but died trying going down face first in a hail of bullets. Soon afterwards, a couple of paramedics began to check them all. When examining Beth, one looked to the other shaking his head. The group made their way over to Beth.

"I know I'm dying, but I'm glad I lived to see that creep get his. How do I look?" she asked as she breathed her last. They hung their heads, and were torn from their thoughts when they heard a paramedic say, "he's still alive over here." It was a miracle that Merle's twisted form still held life. Not far away another paramedic said we're losing one over here, it was Amanda.

Chapter 22

They ended up in a distant Wyoming Hospital being told how lucky they were to be alive and how every alphabet agency was in search for them after discovering the school bus accident along with the man eating hear that went on a rampage terrorizing the country side leaving bodies in its wake. These departments joined together to find the survivors and dispose of the demented bear. It was that outpost fire that helped us with your location. Those who went through the tragic ordeal knew luck had nothing to do with it. Almighty God brought them through this painful experience. Amanda was close to death due to blood loss. Turns out Tabby tested for the same blood type and was more than willing to give Amanda her blood. The others all go stitches, some more than others along with some shots.

*

A year and a half later Tabby invited all of them to come visit her, she had moved to their state Colorado after she sold everything to some big company for 1 billion dollars. Tabby and Keith had gotten married and wanted their friends Michael and Amanda, and Hank and Mae to come see the new log cabin house she had built in Colorado on the lake. Tabby and Keith flew their bush plain that had floats for landing in water. Everyone was in the plain even though they all lived in Colorado; three hundred miles separated Keith and Tabby from them. They landed on the lake in front of this huge beautiful log cabin home. Tabby and Keith began to show them all around the spacious home. It had three levels to it with six bedrooms and four bathrooms. Keith did some bragging about his big grill out on their porch along with the smoker. Tabby had horses with a large barn.

"We have twelve horses and I'd like for us to take a ride. Me and Keith would like to show you something," said Amanda.

"Girl I'm game to go, but I don't know how to ride," said Mae.

"You can ride double with me," said Hank.

"I think your gonna want to get the hang of riding real soon Mae."

"Why you say that?"

"You'll see," Tabby replied.

Once they were on the horses' going along the trail Amanda asked," so how is the married life you too?"

"With Keith's snoring it has its highs and lows, but on a whole it's wonderful." They couldn't help but to laugh.

"I hear y'all getting ready to step off into matrimony," said Tabby.

"Yeah me and Hank been working and saving, maybe by the end of this year we'll have enough saved to buy a home," replied Michael.

The trail kept them along the bank of the lake until they came across an enormous log cabin house just like Keith's and Tabby's and they all dismounted.

"This is why I told you Mae that you will need to learn how to ride a horse. Surprise this is you and Hank's and a mile farther down the lake Amanda and Michael yelled you have one like it too!

"You mean!" Hank was without words and Mae started to fan herself. Amanda's eyes were as wide as food plates and Michael couldn't believe what he just heard.

"What...? What did you say?" He asked.

"You heard her right my friends, we had you one built just like ours at the same time." You could say our homes are triplets. If you look across the lake here you can see Amanda's and Michael's right across over there and ours right over there. We have food and supplies brought by plane once a month and just like my miss said we are only a mile apart.

Mae, Amanda, Michael, and Hank were overjoyed with solar panels and windmill power. Weapons to hunt with and keep them safe, computers and satellite phones to keep them connected to the world, along with a conventional and modern way of living. Tabby told the group to look all around them, letting them know as far they could see the land was all of theirs. Her biggest surprise was giving them account books with five million dollars apiece in them. Everyone was elated, giving many thanks, but Tabby reminded them that they all made this possible. Later that night around the campfire each couple was hugged up with love in their eyes speaking on those they lost along the way and how they would send the families money and keep their memories alive. Amanda, Michael, Mae, Hank, Tabitha, and Keith did a prayer thanking God for being blessed to have each other as

friends and for bringing them out of harm's way.

If you would like to contact the author personally

about this book, please send your emails to

contactus@mocypublishing.com and

Mr. Nolan "Dino" Hall will contact you as soon

as possible. Thank you!

www.ingramcontent.com/pod-product-compliance
Lightning Source LLC
Chambersburg PA
CBHW060529260626
47161CB00003B/824